"Must be a hell of a way to live," she said.

"What do you mean?" he asked, as he put his hands on Earl to hold him down. One hand was on his injured shoulder, the other on his chest. It brought the two of them into very close proximity, and he could smell her. She smelled fresh enough, but there was something else . . . and then he got it. She smelled like sex. Either she'd had sex recently, or this situation was getting her excited.

"I mean being afraid to be without your gun, even when you're in the room with a woman and an injured boy."

"Anyone can pull a trigger, Mrs. Augustus."

"Just call me Gloria," she said, "and hold him steady. If he jerks too hard I could end up killing him."

"I've got him."

She'd been probing for the bullet. At first Earl screamed and bit down on the belt, then he tried to buck. Clint held him down firmly, and the boy passed out.

"He fainted," she said, "that's good. But continue to hold him down just in case."

He did. She started to sweat. It popped out on her head and began to stain the dress under her arms. The odor was pungent, and sexy, and now it was he who was getting excited. He wondered if anyone would mind if he threw her down on the floor and took her when she was done.

He didn't think she'd mind, but her husband might.

DON'T MISS THESE
ALL-ACTION WESTERN SERIES
FROM THE BERKLEY PUBLISHING GROUP

THE GUNSMITH by J. R. Roberts

Clint Adams was a legend among lawmen, outlaws, and ladies. They called him . . . the Gunsmith.

LONGARM by Tabor Evans

The popular long-running series about Deputy U.S. Marshal Long—his life, his loves, his fight for justice.

SLOCUM by Jake Logan

Today's longest-running action Western. John Slocum rides a deadly trail of hot blood and cold steel.

BUSHWHACKERS by B. J. Lanagan

An action-packed series by the creators of Longarm! The rousing adventures of the most brutal gang of cutthroats ever assembled—Quantrill's Raiders.

DIAMONDBACK by Guy Brewer

Dex Yancey is Diamondback, a Southern gentleman turned con man when his brother cheats him out of the family fortune. Ladies love him. Gamblers hate him. But nobody pulls one over on Dex . . .

WILDGUN by Jack Hanson

The blazing adventures of mountain man Will Barlow—from the creators of Longarm!

TEXAS TRACKER by Tom Calhoun

Meet J.T. Law: the most relentless—and dangerous—man-hunter in all Texas. Where sheriffs and posses fail, he's the best man to bring in the most vicious outlaws—for a price.

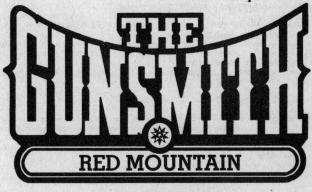

THE GUNSMITH

RED MOUNTAIN

J. R. ROBERTS

JOVE BOOKS, NEW YORK

THE BERKLEY PUBLISHING GROUP
Published by the Penguin Group
Penguin Group (USA) Inc.
375 Hudson Street, New York, New York 10014, USA
Penguin Group (Canada), 90 Eglinton Avenue East, Suite 700, Toronto, Ontario M4P 2Y3, Canada
(a division of Pearson Penguin Canada Inc.)
Penguin Books Ltd., 80 Strand, London WC2R 0RL, England
Penguin Group Ireland, 25 St. Stephen's Green, Dublin 2, Ireland (a division of Penguin Books Ltd.)
Penguin Group (Australia), 250 Camberwell Road, Camberwell, Victoria 3124, Australia
(a division of Pearson Australia Group Pty. Ltd.)
Penguin Books India Pvt. Ltd., 11 Community Centre, Panchsheel Park, New Delhi—110 017, India
Penguin Group (NZ), Cnr. Airborne and Rosedale Roads, Albany, Auckland 1310, New Zealand
(a division of Pearson New Zealand Ltd.)
Penguin Books (South Africa) (Pty.) Ltd., 24 Sturdee Avenue, Rosebank, Johannesburg 2196,
South Africa

Penguin Books Ltd., Registered Offices: 80 Strand, London WC2R 0RL, England

This is a work of fiction. Names, characters, places, and incidents either are the product of the author's imagination or are used fictitiously, and any resemblance to actual persons, living or dead, business establishments, events, or locales is entirely coincidental.

RED MOUNTAIN

A Jove Book / published by arrangement with the author

PRINTING HISTORY
Jove edition / October 2006

Copyright © 2006 by Robert J. Randisi.

ISBN: 0-515-14206-9

JOVE®
Jove Books are published by The Berkley Publishing Group,
a division of Penguin Group (USA) Inc.,
375 Hudson Street, New York, New York 10014.
JOVE is a registered trademark of Penguin Group (USA) Inc.
The "J" design is a trademark belonging to Penguin Group (USA) Inc.

PRINTED IN THE UNITED STATES OF AMERICA

10 9 8 7 6 5 4 3 2 1

ONE

"What's the name of this town?" the man asked the naked woman. "Hoo-ray?"

The girl released the man's rigid penis from her mouth and looked up at him.

"No," she said. "It's Ouray." She emphasized the "oh" when she said "Ooh-ray."

"That's a pretty weird name for a town," he said, staring out the window.

"Are you really interested in what we're doin'?" she asked.

He looked down at her. She was young, but wasn't very pretty. Her nose was too big and her eyes were set too close together. But his friend, Chapman, had recommended her to him when he learned that Hangnil would be going to Ouray.

"Just keep at it," he told her.

"Besides," she muttered, "why's a guy named Hangnail commentin' on a funny name for a town?"

"My name is Hangnil," he said. "Hang-*nil*. Not Hang-*nail*. Just keep suckin', whore!"

The whore's name was Rosetta. Oh, that wasn't her real name, that was her "stage" name. She imagined that one day she was going to be a great actress, and she would appear on stage under that single name—Rosetta. Right now, her job was seeing to the sexual needs of the miners, but that would change.

She decided to give this miner something to remember. Usually when she gave a miner a sucking it was over quick and they were real appreciative. A lot of the girls in the Bird Cage wouldn't do that. They thought it was disgusting, especially with a filthy miner. Rosetta didn't mind, though. She would actually rather have a miner in her mouth than in her pussy.

This fella, though, this Hang-nail, he was busy staring out the window while she was sucking him. That was an insult. Usually when she did that to a man his eyes rolled up into his head. So now she decided she was going to give this guy a royal sucking. She took his penis into her hand, stroked it a few times, then slid it into her mouth. Luckily, it wasn't very big so it was easy to accommodate. She'd had lots bigger men than this in her mouth. As she started to suck him again she made it good and wet, and fondled his testicles while she did it. When she heard him moan she knew he was through looking out the window for a while. She began to bob up and down on his dick faster and faster and slid her hands around so that she was cupping his naked, hairy ass.

When he finally shot off into her mouth he bellowed like a bull, filling her not only with his jism but with a great deal of pride, as well.

She was really good at this.

As Hangnil bellied up to the Bird Cage bar he thought again what a funny name this place had. No matter what the whore said, it sounded like "Hoo-ray," to him. The whore, she'd turned out to be pretty good. He'd have to thank his buddy Chapman for recommending her, when he got back to Red Mountain Town. Now there was a funny name for a town, too. Why not just call it Red Mountain? Why put the word "town" after it? Everybody knew it was a town. Of course, the funniest name for a town up here in the San Juan mountains was Sneffles. He and his friends always called it Sniffles and thought they were real clever.

"Whataya have?" the bartender asked.

"Beer."

His knees were still shaking from the sucking that whore had given him. After this beer he was going to get him some food. The fella he was supposed to be meeting was coming to town today, so he contented himself with the thought that he'd be back in Red Mountain by tomorrow. This Hooray or Ouray or whatever was too big for him. Mining towns oughtn't get this big, he thought. He'd heard-tell there was a couple of thousand people here now. That wasn't a mining town anymore, it was a goddamned city. Must have been that many people in Denver, for Chrissake, although he'd never been to Denver so he didn't know for sure.

"Was you upstairs with Rosetta just now?"

For a moment he thought the bartender was speaking to him, because the man was setting his beer down in front of him. But then the man withdrew and he realized it was a fella standing next to him who had spoken.

"Huh?" he said, picking up his beer.

"Rosetta," the man said. "You was just with her?"

He looked the man up and down. Didn't look like much, mid-twenties, maybe, dirty trail clothes and a worn six-gun on his hip.

"What if I was?"

"She give you a suck?"

"What the hell—"

"Most of these girls don't do that," the young man said, "but she does. She likes it, I reckon."

Hangnil sipped his beer and tried to ignore the man. It seemed more like he was talking to himself, anyway.

"I'm talkin' to you."

"I don't know you, friend," Hangnil said. "I'm just tryin' ta drink my beer."

Suddenly, the man poked him in the arm with the forefinger of his left hand. Hangnil didn't see it, but the man's other hand was on his gun. Hangnil was a miner. He didn't carry a gun, although that was the other piece of advice Chapman had given him. Get a suck from Rosetta, his friend had said, and carry a gun.

"There's lots of people down there," Chapman had said, "and some of them is crazy."

But Hangnil didn't like guns, so he didn't carry

one. Besides, what reason would anyone have for shooting him? He kept to himself and didn't bother anyone.

But when the man had poked him in the arm he'd ended up spilling some beer down the front of his shirt.

"Hey, goddamnit!" he swore.

"Rosetta's my girl, ya know?" the man said.

"What the hell—" Hangnil put his beer down and turned to face the man, who was about half a foot shorter than his own six-four. Hangnil was tall and lanky and was not a man quick to anger. He didn't like to fight because, despite his height, he usually got whupped because he carried very little weight on him. But he'd been looking forward to that beer and now some of it was running down his shirt. Not only would he not be able to drink those precious drops of beer, but he looked silly.

"Go fer yer gun," the younger man said.

"I ain't got a g—" Hangnil started, but before he could finish the shorter man pulled his gun and shot him in the chest.

Damn, Hangnil thought as he fell backwards, all I wanted was a suck and a beer . . .

TWO

As Clint Adams rode into the town of Ouray he was impressed. He liked mining towns because they were filled with so much energy. It was not only the miners, but everyone else who was attracted to the town. The storekeepers, the gamblers, the businessmen and businesswomen—which usually meant whores—the flimflam artists, drummers, newspapermen, they all turned out for a good strike and this one happened to be gold. It had been over ten years since the first strike in Ouray, and just recently the railroad had made it to town. Ouray had become a hub for all the surrounding mining camps and towns, and Clint had been told that the population had swelled to almost two thousand. Now, riding down Second Street, he could believe it. There were people everywhere, walking, running, driving buckboards, and a lot of them seemed to be running towards the Bird Cage Saloon.

"What's going on?" he asked a youngster who was running past him.

"Fella got hisself shot in the Bird Cage!" the boy replied.

"Is that unusual?" he shouted, but the boy was gone, eager to get his look at spilled blood.

Shootings were not unusual in any town, although there were fewer than there used to be in major cities like Denver and San Francisco. Law had become so organized, with police departments instead of just sheriffs and marshals. This was a mining town, though, no matter how big it might have grown, and it was likely the law here was a sheriff.

Still, the shooting was no concern of his. He needed to board his Darley Arabian, Eclipse, and get himself a hotel room before he went in search of a meal. After that he'd look for the man who was supposed to meet him and then he'd find out what the hell he was doing in the town of Ouray.

Sheriff Henry Buckles stared down at the body of the dead miner, shaking his head.

"And you say Arvard just shot 'im?"

"Just pulled his gun and shot 'im dead, where he stood, Sheriff," the bartender said.

There was a crowd still standing around the sheriff and the body and Buckles turned to look at them.

"Anybody know this fella?"

Lots of "no's" and shaking heads.

"Well, he's obviously a miner," he said, looking at

the bartender. "What was he talkin' to Arvard about, Walter?"

"Rosetta."

"Aw, Jeez—"

"I'm gonna have ta let 'er go," Walter Gibson said. "I can't have Arvard shootin' every customer that's with her."

"This is the first one, ain't it?"

"First one he's shot," Walter said. "He's wailed on a few."

"Ain't the gal's fault, Walter," Buckles said. "Don't let him in here anymore."

"Well, I figure he won't be around no more," Walter said. "I mean, not after you arrest 'im."

"I gotta find 'im before I arrest 'im." He looked at the crowd again. "Anybody know where Arvard is?"

A lot of shrugs and head shakes.

"Okay, then it's time to break it up," the sheriff said. "Go back to your drinkin' or card playin'. Ain't nothin' left here ta see."

As the crowd began to disperse he spotted two men and said, "Larry, you and Denny get this body out of here."

"Where do we take it? Doc's?"

"He's dead, ain't he?" the lawman asked. "What the hell is Doc gonna be able ta do for him? Take him to the undertaker's."

Grumbling, the two men grabbed the dead miner's feet and shoulders and hauled him out of the saloon.

"Better get somebody ta wash that blood off the floor, Walter," Buckles said.

"I'll soak in," Walter said. "It always does."

"Don't be so hard on that gal, Walter," Buckles said. "Ya know she does things the other girls won't do."

"I know," Walter said. "She's one of my top earners. Well, if you get that crazy Arvard off the streets I won't have ta let 'er go."

"I'll do my best," Buckles said. "Walter you ever been with that gal yerself?"

"Me? You crazy? Don't lay with no whores. Ya know what kind of diseases they carry?"

"I was just wonderin', ya know? I mean . . . what she does that's so special?"

Walter smiled at the lawman, revealing gaps in several places. They had a dentist in town who thought the cure for everything was to pull a tooth. Buckles didn't go anywhere near the man.

"Pay yer money and find out, Sheriff."

"Yeah," Buckles said. He and Walter were about the same age, mid-fifties, and had come to Ouray around the same time. They were friends, but not so friendly that Walter would give his girls away for free. "Maybe another time."

He turned to leave, then turned back.

"Walter, you think Rosetta would know where Arvard is?"

"She don't wanna have nothin' ta do with him, Sheriff," Walter said. "Ever since the first time he was with her all he's done is cause trouble. I don't think she'd have any ideas."

"Okay," Buckles said. He looked around the place,

which seemed to have gotten back to normal after the shooting. "I'll be seein' ya."

"Them miners come to town to find out what happened to one of theirs, you tell 'em I had nothin' ta do with it. I don't want them comin' here ta cause trouble."

"I'll tell 'em," Buckles promised. "With a little luck I can have Arvard in a cell by the time they get here."

"That poor fella waren't even armed!" Walter called out as the sheriff went out through the batwing doors.

Arvard Turner had been nothing but trouble since he first came to Ouray several years before. He fancied himself a gunman, often threatened men with his professed prowess, usually in some sort of dispute over Rosetta, who Arvard had apparently fallen in love with after being with her once. But this was the first time he'd actually gone and shot someone. Unfortunately for him it happened to be a miner, and an unarmed one, to boot.

It was time to take Arvard off the streets of Ouray and put him in a cage.

THREE

Clint found the livery stable—or *a* livery stable. In a town of this size there had to be more than one. Anyway, the liveryman was properly impressed with Eclipse and promised to take good care of him. He then recommended the Beaumont Hotel.

"Fella with a horse like this ought to be used to the best," he told Clint. "The Beaumont is the best hotel in Colorado . . . west of Denver, anyway."

"Thanks," Clint said, hefting his saddlebags and rifle. "I'll look into it."

"Don't be put off by them ladies groups that meet there in the afternoon," the man told him. "There's plenty in the Beaumont to make a fella happy."

"Good food?"

"The best steak in town."

"Sold," Clint said. "Thanks a lot."

He left the livery and headed down the street, following the man's directions to the Beaumont Hotel.

•   •   •

Sheriff Buckles watched from the boardwalk as Larry and Denny carried the dead miner across the street. Then he noticed a fella heading towards him carrying his saddlebags and rifle. He didn't need those things to tell him this was a stranger, though. Buckles prided himself on knowing who belonged and who didn't in Ouray, in spite of its size.

"Sheriff," the fella said, by way of greeting.

"Afternoon. Just get to town?"

"That's right," the man said. "Heard there was a shooting."

"Miner got himself killed over a girl," Buckles said.

"In here?" The man looked at the front of the Bird Cage.

"That's right. You headed in there?"

"Maybe later," the man said. "If the beer's cold."

"It is."

"I've got to get myself a hotel room, first. Fella at the livery recommended the Beaumont. That a good place?"

"Best in town," the sheriff said. "Yer gonna need to have some money, though."

"Well, I'm not a rich man, but I can usually afford the best for myself."

"Passin' through, or you plannin' on stayin' a while?" Buckles asked him.

"I'm not sure," Clint said.

"Business or pleasure?"

"To tell you the truth I'm not sure of that, either."

"You got a name?"

"Adams," Clint said. He set down his saddlebags and extended his hand. "Clint Adams."

Buckles hesitated, then shook Clint's hand.

"Henry Buckles," he said. "Been sheriff here since day one, when this town was nothin' but tents and mud puddles."

Clint looked at the street, which was still pretty much a collection of mud puddles.

"Mines around here must be pretty rich to support a town for this long."

"Ain't no sign of them peterin' out anytime soon."

"That's good," Clint said, picking up his saddlebags. "I guess I'll be seeing you around."

"I'll be around," Buckles said, "me or one of my deputies. Man with your rep, Mr. Adams, you wouldn't be bringin' trouble here with you, would ya?"

"Sheriff," Clint said, "looks to me like you had plenty of trouble here already without any help from me."

"Guess you got that right."

"Well, I don't aim to be adding to it for you," Clint said. "I'll just keep to myself."

"Sounds like a good idea, Mr. Adams," Buckles said. "If you'll excuse me, I got me a killer to catch."

"Good luck to you."

Buckles stepped down into the wet street and walked across it. Clint watched as the man splashed through mud puddles as if he didn't care they were there.

It reminded him that he needed a bath.

FOUR

"It ain't my fault he killed a fella over me!" Rosetta shouted at Walter Gibson.

"You just gotta be more careful with these men, girl," he warned. "Don't make 'em think yer in love with 'em or nothin' like that."

Rosetta, whose real name was a much less fancy Gladys Williams, said, "All I do is give 'em their money's worth, Walter. That's what you want, ain't it?"

"Well . . . yer givin' 'em somethin' the other girls ain't, that's for sure," he said, shakin' his head. "The sheriff wanted to know if you knew where Arvard lives?"

"I don't know nothin' about Arvard except that he's crazy about me," she said. "And just plain crazy. You ever look into his eyes? They're sure scary. You can't be lettin' fellers like that in here, Walter. It don't make the girls feel safe."

"I can't exactly stop fellas from comin' into the Bird Cage because of what their eyes look like."

"Well, then, you need some more security."

"Yeah, well, mebbee you're right about that," he admitted.

"At least take their guns," she said. "It's real hard for the girls to concentrate when they think a feller might shoot 'em."

"Takin' a man's gun from him ain't an easy thing, girl," he said, "especially not in a mining town."

"Well, that miner didn't have no gun."

"And look what happened ta him," Walter said. "Okay, I'll have ta think on this some."

"So you ain't gonna fire me?"

"Hell, no, I ain't gonna fire ya," he said. Walter looked her up and down. He had several girls who were prettier than her, but what was special about her was obviously not in her looks. Maybe, he thought, maybe he should put aside his rule of not sleeping with whores and try her out.

Abruptly, she stepped in and hugged him, pressing her small breasts against him.

"Thanks Walter. I really need this job."

Flustered he said, "Yeah, well, okay." He didn't know what to do with his hands, but eventually he put them on her thin shoulders and pushed her away from him gently. "I got to get back ta work."

"Me, too."

"You sure you don't wanna take a break after what happened?" he asked.

"Naw," she said. "Just send the next feller up."

"Okay, then," he said. "It so happens I got one down there just chompin' at the bit."

"I'm ready."

Walter nodded, backed out of her room and closed the door gently.

In point of fact, Rosetta found it sort of thrilling that one man had killed another man over her. She just wished it hadn't been that crazy Arvard killin' that poor miner feller. At least she'd managed to show that miner a real good time before he died.

She looked around her room, which was as neat as she could keep it, what with men coming in and out all day. Walter had a lot of girls working for him, some just saloon girls, others prostitutes like her, and some of them doing both jobs. She preferred to do one job and do it well, and she really didn't fancy being on her feet as long as saloon girls had to be. She also didn't want to have to spend her money on those fancy dresses.

There was a knock on her door then and she could tell it wasn't a feller.

"Come in."

The door opened and her best friend, Monica, stuck her pretty blond head in.

"Just wanted to check and see if you was all right, hon," her friend said.

Monica was just about the prettiest whore in town. Between the two of them they got most of the men. Like her, Monica had her own plans for the future.

She wanted to own her own whorehouse, so that all she'd do was take the money while other girls did the work.

The blonde opened the door wide and stood in the doorway. Even Rosetta was taken by her beauty. She had a full, womanly body with pale skin and large breasts, almost like white globes that—like today—were usually spilling out the top of her dress. Sometimes, Monica put on a nice dress and went down to work the saloon floor. She was beautiful enough to do that, and she looked real nice in those dresses. Rosetta wondered if she had a body like Monica would she be doing that, too?

"That crazy Arvard," Monica said. "I was down there when it happened. He shot that miner dead with no warning. Poor guy."

"I didn't even get his name," Rosetta said. "Just gave him a good sucking and sent him on his way."

"Well, maybe he died with a smile on his face."

Monica was the only other girl in the house who pleasured men with her mouth. However, she freely admitted that she wasn't as good at it as Rosetta was. She got most of the men she did with her body and her beautiful face.

"Walter give you some time off?" she asked.

"He offered, but I tol' him ta send the next feller up. Should be here any minute."

"Well, then, I'll get outta your hair. Got me a feller comin' up, too. Supper together later?"

"Sure."

"See ya, hon." Monica said, and flounced out, closing the door behind her.

They were friends despite the fact that Monica was about ten years older than Rosetta's twenty-three years. The blonde told Rosetta she wanted her to work for her when she got her own house, but Rosetta always said that she'd be on the stage by then. She knew Monica would eventually get her own place, though, so it was nice to know she'd have something to fall back on.

She stopped thinking about her future when there was a heavy knock on her door, signaling that the next feller was ready for his turn.

FIVE

Clint was impressed with the Beaumont Hotel. Although on a smaller scale, it presented many of the qualities of some of the hotels he'd stayed at in Denver and San Francisco. The lobby was large, well furnished, and smelled of leather and cleaning solution. Despite the muddy street out front, the floors were clean. The management obviously went to the trouble of keeping it that way.

He checked in and collected his key from the desk clerk, who greeted him cordially and outlined all the amenities available to him. The two that appealed to him most at the moment were a bath and a meal. Throw in a cold beer and things would be perfect.

His room was large, the bed comfortable, the furniture of good quality. It would have taken many trips with a buckboard to get the stuff over the mountains. Someone was very determined to make this hotel a success. Probably someone who knew or suspected that the railroad would soon be coming in, making Ouray more than just another mining town that would eventually dry up and blow away, like many had done before.

After a quick bath—hunger would not allow him to linger in the hot water—he went down to the Beaumont dining room and ordered a steak. It came with all the trimmings and, to top it all off, an ice-cold beer. While he ate the perfectly prepared steak, he took out the telegram, which was the reason he was there. Briefly, it asked if he would come to the mining town of Ouray, Colorado, in the San Juan Mountains—a place he had previously never heard of—where he would be met by a man who would then take him to a place called Red Mountain Town. He thought Bat may have sent the telegram and hoped he would explain the reasons for bringing him to Ouray when he arrived.

He would wait until morning to see if anyone approached him. If not, he was sure he could secure directions to Red Mountain Town and get there himself. He did wonder why Bat wouldn't come to Ouray himself to get him, but that would be explained, also.

Meanwhile, the steak he was eating was almost reason enough to have ridden all the way from Texas to get there, so he decided to devote his entire attention to finishing what was left of it.

"What's that?" Sheriff Buckles asked.

"A piece of paper," Ira Weldon, the undertaker, said.

"Why are you givin' it to me?"

"Because I took it out of the dead man's pocket," Weldon said, "and it has a name written on it."

"Is it his name?"

"I doubt it."

"Why?"

"Because I recognize the name," Weldon said, "and I doubt that this is the same man."

Buckles took the piece of paper and looked at it.

"Damn it," he said.

Written on the slip of paper was the name Clint Adams.

Clint was working on a piece of peach pie when the sheriff appeared in the dining room doorway and looked around. He knew the man was looking for him. He could feel it. With relatively few diners present the man spotted him right away and came walking over.

"Didn't expect to see you again so soon, Sheriff," he said.

"Likewise, Adams."

"Have a seat."

Buckles sat across from Clint.

"Coffee?"

"No, thanks." The lawman tossed a slip of paper on the table between them. Clint could see that it bore his name in a scrawled handwriting he didn't recognize.

"What's this?"

"That fella I told you got shot today?"

"Yeah."

"He had this on him. You wanna tell me why you're in town five minutes and already a dead man's got your name in his pocket?"

Clint picked up the slip, eyed it for a moment, then set it down in a coffee stain.

"I was supposed to be met by somebody today," Clint said. "Maybe by the dead man. You got a name for him?"

"Not yet. How about you come to the undertaker's and have a look at him?"

"I can do that, but I don't know how much help I'll be. I doubt I'll recognize him."

"Why?"

"Well, if he had my name in his pocket, we probably didn't know each other."

The sheriff frowned. It was a good point.

"Have a look anyway, if you would."

"Sure," Clint said. "Can I finish my pie first?"

"Why not?"

Clint followed the sheriff to the undertaker's office, where they took him in the back to have a look at the dead man.

"Know 'im?" Buckles asked.

"Never saw him before. Why was he killed?"

"Argument over a woman, is what I heard," Ira Weldon said.

"A whore," Buckles said. "Argument over a whore."

"Was he armed?" Clint asked.

"No."

"Somebody shot him over a whore and he wasn't even armed?" Clint asked. "Anybody know who did it?"

"Everybody knows," Buckles said. "Everybody in the saloon saw it. Fella named Arvard Turner. Fancies himself a gunman."

"Not much of a gunman if he had to shoot an unarmed man," Clint observed. "You arrest him?"

"I will," the sheriff said. "As soon as I can find him."

Clint looked at the man again. There was nothing remarkable about him.

"Sorry I couldn't help," he said.

"That's okay," the lawman said. "Thanks for havin' a look."

"Mind if I go now? I had my mouth set for another cold beer after my steak."

"No," Buckles said. "Go ahead."

"Any reason I shouldn't have that beer at the Bird Cage?"

"Biggest place in town," the sheriff said. "Don't see why not."

"Prefer Carrie's Place myself," the undertaker said. "The Bird Cage is a little too . . . lively for me."

Clint looked at the undertaker, who appeared to be in his late sixties.

"Think I'll chance it," he said and left.

SIX

Clint passed Carrie's Place during his walk from the undertaker's to the Bird Cage. Also a place called the Clipper and a few other establishments. The Bird Cage, while nothing like the Bird Cage in Tombstone, was easily the biggest place in town. There was a sign by the door in the front announcing that beer and whores could be had inside. Clint wondered which of them carried the higher price. Probably the whores, since one of them had apparently been worth killing a man over.

He entered and found the place filled to the rafters with men—gamblers, miners, drummers and drifters, he figured. There were some girls in worn dresses working the floor. He made his way to the long bar and elbowed a space for himself. Along the way he passed what looked like a bloodstain in the floor.

"What can I get ya?" the bartender asked.

"Beer."

"Comin' up."

The man drew him a mug and returned, setting it down in front of him.

"How about a girl today?"

"No, thanks," Clint said. "I hear your girls are dangerous."

"Dangerous?"

"Heard somebody got shot over one."

The man's face fell.

"Oh, that. I knew that was gonna cost me some business."

Clint grabbed the beer and found it ice cold.

"Maybe this'll get some back for you," he said, taking a good swallow.

"You're a stranger in town," the bartended said, "and you already heard about it."

"Doesn't look like it's hurt you any, today."

"Not so far. How'd you hear about it?"

"Seems the dead man had my name in his pocket."

"Huh?"

"That's what I said," Clint replied. He took another swallow of beer and set it down. "Did anybody know the dead miner?"

"Naw," the barman said. "Other miners won't be here till later, when they get off shift."

"None of these fellas were miners?"

"Not from up the mountain," the man said. "That feller, he was from Red Mountain, or Sneffles, I reckon. Those boys won't be along until later. Maybe one of them will know him."

The bartender moved away to serve some other

customers and Clint stared into his beer. He'd come here on a whim. He could have ignored the telegram, but the truth was he'd been bored for a while. The telegram had found him in Labyrinth, Texas, where he was going stir crazy, so he took the opportunity to ride to Colorado and check out a town he'd never been to before.

And walked right into the middle of a killing, first day, first hour—hell, first ten minutes he was there.

SEVEN

"Here they come," the bartender said to Clint hours later.

Clint had literally decided to remain in the Bird Cage until some of the miners began showing up. He had a few beers and played small stakes poker with some of the town merchants and a drummer. He was the only one winning not only because he was the best player, but because the drummer kept up a steady patter, trying to sell his wares to the merchants, thereby distracting everyone—including himself—from his cards.

The bartender had walked over to Clint's table, leaned over and spoke. Clint looked at the door, through which five men had entered together. They were all dressed as miners. Three of the five were unarmed, but the other two had pistols stuck into their belts.

As the men marched to the bar and ordered their

27

drinks Clint cashed out of his small game and stood up. The drummer was still talking and he doubted any of them noticed he was gone. But just as he was about to approach the men the batwing doors swung inward once again and the sheriff entered, followed by a younger man wearing a deputy's badge. Instead of approaching the miners, Clint instead approached the two lawmen.

"Looks like we had the same idea, Sheriff," he said.

"Except that talkin' to them miners is my job, Adams, not yours," Sheriff Buckles said.

"Maybe not my job," Clint said, "but I'd like to find out the name of the man who was supposed to be meeting me here—if only to try to find out who sent him."

"You don't know who sent him?"

"I just said that."

"Why would you come here, then?"

"I've been asking myself the same question, Sheriff . . ."

Rick Hartman had asked Clint the same thing before he left Labyrinth, Texas.

"Why would you ride all that way because of a telegram that's not even signed?" Rick asked. "You don't need the thousand dollars. Or if you do, I'll give it to you."

"I don't need the money, you're right," Clint said.

They were sitting in Hartman's saloon and gambling house, Rick's Place.

"I'm bored, Rick," he'd said. "Pure and simple."

"Boredom can kill you," Rick said, "in more ways than one . . ."

Clint knew his friend was right. Many men had died in the name of boredom or curiosity. He himself had come close more than a time or two.

"And what's yer answer?" Buckles asked.

"I'll let you know."

"All right, then," the lawman said, "you might as well come along. This is my deputy, Harve Parker. Harve, Clint Adams."

The young man swallowed and said, "P-pleased ta meet you, Mr. Adams."

"You, too, Deputy."

"Just keep quiet and let me do the talkin'," Buckles told Clint.

"I won't make a sound."

"And keep your hand away from yer gun."

Clint put his hands out and waggled his fingers.

"Come on."

Buckles approached the men at the bar with the deputy and Clint behind him.

"You men mind if I talk to ya for a minute?" he asked.

The five men turned and eyed Buckles, then Clint and the deputy.

"We ain't done nothin', Sheriff," one of the two armed men said. "We just came in for a friendly drink."

"I know ya ain't done nothin'," Buckles said. "I just need ta ask ya about a miner who was killed here earlier today."

Now the five men turned and faced Buckles.

"A miner got killed today? How?" the spokesman asked.

"Got hisself shot over a gal," Buckles said.

"Goddamn," one of the others said.

"Well," a third said, "if ya gotta go . . . was she pretty?"

"Shut up, Lem," the spokesman said. "Sheriff, my name's Dan Chapman. A friend of mine came to town today to run an errand. I sent him here to see one of the girls. Is that when he got killed?"

"Well," Buckles said, "the dead man did see one of the gals here before he got killed, but we don't know his name."

"Hangnil," Chapman said, "his name's Ben Hangnil."

"Well, he didn't have anythin' on him that said his name," Buckles responded. "He did have this feller's name on him, though."

Chapman looked at Clint.

"Who're you?"

"Clint Adams," he said. "The dead man had my name written on a slip of paper. You know anything about that?"

"I only know that Ben said he had to come to town to run an errand for somebody," Chapman said. "That's all he told me."

"Maybe you'd better come over to the under-taker's to see if we're talkin' about the same man."

"Sure thing. Boys, the rest of you stay here. I'll be back."

"Dan," one of them said, "you got the money—"

"Just stay here and drink your beer," Chapman said. "You can go upstairs later." He turned back to Buckles. "Sheriff, lead the way."

"That's him," Chapman said, looking down at the dead man. "That's Ben Hangnil."

They stood quietly for a few moments, and then Sheriff Buckles said, "I'm sorry about your friend."

"I told him to carry a gun," Chapman said. "He wouldn't listen."

"Don't know that it woulda helped," Buckles said.

Chapman turned and glared at the lawman. Clint saw the burning light of vengeance in his eyes. He'd seen it in men before.

"Who did it?" Chapman asked. "Who shot him?"

"Fella named Arvard Turner," the sheriff said.

"That turd?"

"You know him?"

"I've seen him around," Chapman said. "Fancies himself a gunman. Guess he ain't above shooting an unarmed man. Where do I find him?"

"What for?"

"Just tell me."

"If I knew where to find him, he'd be in a cell right now."

"Well, when I find him you won't have to worry about locking him up."

"Now wait a minute—"

"I ain't got a minute," Chapman said and stormed out.

"Shit," Buckles said. "More trouble. Stay on him, Harve."

"Want me to lock him up, Sheriff?"

"Just follow him, see where he goes. Keep him out of trouble if you can."

"Mind if I tag along with the deputy, Sheriff?"

"What for?"

"I still need to find out something about this man that might help me."

"You gonna talk to Chapman?"

"I thought I might."

"Then you go instead," the sheriff said. "Talk to him, convince him to leave this to me."

"He's a young man, Sheriff," Clint said. Not in his twenties like Deputy Parker, but certainly his early thirties. "You know what it's like to be young and lose a friend, don't you?"

"Yeah, I do," Buckles said. "That's why I wanna keep him out of trouble."

"Well," Clint said. "He doesn't know me from a hole in the ground, but I'll see what I can do."

"If anybody can warn him about trouble," Buckles said. "It's you. You sure seen your fair share."

Clint couldn't argue with that.

EIGHT

Clint caught up to Chapman in front of the Bird Cage and called out the man's name.

"Yeah?" Chapman asked, turning.

"Can I talk to you a minute?"

"You gonna try to talk me outta killing this fella Turner?" Chapman asked.

"You can kill him if you want," Clint said. "It's no skin off my nose."

"Then what do you want?"

"I want to know about your friend, Hangnil."

"Why?"

"He had my name in his pocket," Clint said. "I knew I was supposed to meet somebody here, but I didn't know who. If it was your friend and he's dead, then now I don't know why I was meeting him. Maybe you can help me."

"I doubt it."

"How about I buy you a drink and we talk about

33

it?" Clint asked. "You've got plenty of time to find Turner and kill him."

"I suppose I do," Chapman said. "In here?" He pointed to the Bird Cage.

"Let's go someplace quieter."

"Okay," Chapman said. "Let's go to Carrie's Place, right down the street."

"I know where it is," Clint said. "I passed it earlier today."

"Let me tell my friends where I'll be," Chapman said. "I'll meet you there."

Clint figured Chapman was also going to give his friends the money he was holding so they could get on with their night.

"Fine."

Clint walked down the street to Carrie's Place and entered. He was struck immediately by the difference between this place and the Bird Cage. While the Cage offered drinks and sex, Carrie's Place was more for gamblers. Oh, there were a few girls working the floor, but all they were selling was drinks. There was a roulette wheel in the center of the room, a faro table in one corner, and any number of poker games going on. The noise level was a lot lower.

He was still standing just inside the door when Chapman entered.

"Big difference, huh?" the man asked.

"This looks like more my kind of place," Clint said.

"You like gambling better than girls?"

"I don't mind paying for my gambling," Clint said, "but I don't pay for girls."

"Let's get a table."

They found one against the wall and a girl came over immediately to see what they wanted.

"What are you doin' here, Chappie?" she asked. "They run short of girls at the Bird Cage."

"Just came in for a quick drink, Lindy," Chapman said. "My friend is buyin', so I'll have a whiskey and a beer."

"I'll have the same,' Clint said, "but hold the whiskey."

"Comin' up," the pretty redhead said.

As she flounced off Chapman looked at Clint and said, "You said your name was Adams?"

"Is Adams," Clint said. "Yeah."

"As in the Gunsmith?"

"That's right."

"And you were supposed to meet with Ben?"

"I guess he was supposed to meet with me," Clint said.

"What for?"

Clint shrugged. "My best guess is that he was supposed to tell me. He didn't mention me to you?"

"No," Chapman said. "He just said that he had to run an errand for somebody."

"He do that sort of thing?"

"No," Chapman said. "Hangnil was a miner. I guess he was doin' somebody a favor."

Lindy came back with their drinks and set them down. Clint paid her and gave her enough extra to earn him a big smile. It was worth it. The smile lit up her face.

"I'll check back with you gents in a while."

"Hangnil was a good friend of yours?" Clint asked.

"He was a friend."

"And yet you're willing to kill over him?"

"How good does a friend have to be for that?" Chapman asked. "I ain't got so many that I can afford to have one of them killed for no reason."

"I can understand that."

Chapman tossed the whiskey back and then chased it with a swallow of beer.

"You don't strike me as a miner," Clint said.

"I wasn't, until I got here," Chapman said. "This was a big strike."

"You working for somebody, or do you have your own claim?"

"Both," Chapman said. "The money I get paid for working in one of the bigger mines lets me work my own claim. It's a small one, but I take enough out of it."

"And Hangnil?"

"He worked in one of the big Red Mountain mines."

"Which one?"

"The Reddick Mining Company, owned by Bill Reddick."

"So Reddick may have sent him to town to meet me."

"What brought you to town in the first place?"

"A telegram."

"Signed by who?"

"Unsigned."

"And you came?"

Instead of trying to explain the reasons, Clint said, "There was the promise of a thousand dollars."

Chapman whistled.

"A thousand? Must've been one of the big companies then. That means either Reddick or Augustus."

"Augustus?"

"Augustus Mining, owned by Jerrod Augustus. Those are the two biggest companies hereabouts."

"And are both companies out of Red Mountain?"

"It's actually called Red Mountain Town, but yeah, both are based there."

"Then I guess I'd better head up there and see if it was one of them that sent for me."

"That's probably the only way you'll see your thousand dollars," Chapman said.

"It's more than the money," Clint said. "Now I'm just damned curious."

"Well, sorry Ben got killed and messed things up for you."

"Look, I'm sorry your friend is dead, but I had nothing to do with that. Unless . . ."

"Unless what?"

"Well . . . what if somebody didn't want him to meet me?"

"You think he was killed to keep him from seein' you? That would mean somebody hired Arvard Turner to gun 'im."

"Just a thought," Clint said. "Has there been any trouble around here?"

"What kind of trouble?"

"Gun play? Friction between the two big mines?"

"There's always been friction between Augustus and Reddick," Chapman said, "but nothin' that ever involved guns."

"I guess I'll just have to find out from them."

Chapman looked thoughtful.

"So if I kill Turner as soon as I see him we may not find out if he was hired."

"I guess . . ." Clint said. "Might be better, then, if you find him, to turn him over to the sheriff."

"Yeah," Dan Chapman said, rubbing his jaw, "yeah, I can see that . . ." He got up from his chair. "I think I'd better go and see to my friends. I usually have to keep them out of trouble."

"Hey, Chapman."

The man stopped and turned to face Clint.

"Yeah?"

"You said you weren't a miner until you came up here."

"That's right."

"What did you do before that?"

Chapman hesitated, then looked down at his gun, which was simply tucked into his belt.

"I made my way with this."

"You hired it?"

Chapman nodded.

"Chapman . . ." Clint repeated. "Chapman . . . should I know your name?"

"Not if I did my job right all those years," Chapman said. "I usually let my gun do the talkin', not my reputation."

As Chapman left, Clint wondered if he'd just been criticized for the way he'd lived his life.

NINE

"One drink was enough for him?"

Clint looked up, saw Lindy standing next to him, smiling at him.

"I guess so," Clint said. "He went back to the Bird Cage to keep his friends out of trouble."

"Get himself into trouble is more like it."

"Something going on between you two?"

"Nope," she said. "Just somebody I see around a lot. I know a lot of the miners by name, but if they want more than that from a gal, they go to the Bird Cage."

"I see."

"What about you?"

"What about me?"

She bumped his shoulder with her hip and asked, "You want more than that?"

"Not bad enough to pay for it."

"Ah . . ." she said.

"*Ah* what?"

"So that makes you different from other men."

"That and a lot more."

"Ah . . ." she said, again. "You want another drink?"

"I'll have another beer, sure."

"Comin' up."

She nudged him with her hip as she turned and walked away. He watched her make her way to the bar, then noticed as the doors opened and the sheriff walked in.

"You following me?" Clint asked as the man reached his table.

"Makin' rounds," Buckles said.

"Have a seat. You just missed Chapman."

"Oh?" Buckles sat across from him. "You have that talk with him?"

"Yeah," Clint said. "I don't think he'll be shooting first and asking questions later."

The lawman looked surprised.

"You talked him out of it?"

"I sort of let him talk himself out of it." He relayed to the man the conversation he'd had with Chapman.

"So you don't really believe that the miner was killed to keep him from talking to you?"

"Well . . . anything's possible, I guess."

"I suppose if anyone around here had the money to hire you, it would be one of those big mines."

"Yeah, but hire me for what?"

"Your gun, naturally," the lawman said. "I mean, ain't that what you do?"

Clint gave the sheriff a hard look and said, "Actually, no, it isn't. I don't hire my gun out."

"Sorry," Buckles said. "It's just . . . well, your reputation."

"My reputation isn't for being a hired gun."

"Sorry."

When Lindy came back she was carrying a beer for each of them.

"Hey, Sheriff."

"Hello, Lindy."

"You fellas friends?"

"No," Clint said, "we just met today."

"Well, the sheriff drinks for free here," she said. "If you were his friend you'd drink free, too."

"That's okay," Clint said. "I'll pay."

"Hey," Buckles said, as Lindy walked away, "I said I was sorry. Ya can't blame me for believin' your reputation."

"I suppose not."

"Anyway, thanks for talkin' to Chapman," Buckles said. "I guess I don't have to worry about him gunnin' Arvard on sight."

"You know what Chapman did for a living before he came here?" Clint asked.

"Yeah, he was a money gun," Buckles said. "Like you . . . like I thought you was."

"Any chance Arvard could outgun him?"

Buckles thought it over.

"I'm not sure," he said, finally. "Arvard's kinda fast, and I ain't never seen Chapman's move. And I never heard that Chapman was a fast gun."

"Arvard ever kill anyone in a fair fight that you know of?" Clint asked.

"No."

"Ever kill anyone before?"

"No."

"Well, then I say no," Clint said. "Using a gun was Chapman's business. Fast or not, if he was any good he knows how to use a gun, and he knows how to kill."

"So we don't have to worry about Arvard killin' Chapman."

"Unless he shoots him in the back," Clint said. "Any man who'd shoot an unarmed man would shoot somebody in the back. Both are the act of a coward."

"Arvard's young, full of himself, foolish . . . yeah, and maybe a coward."

"Most cowards hide behind something," Clint said. "Apparently, he hides behind a gun."

"I can't argue with that." Buckles finished his beer and set the empty mug down. "Gotta finish my rounds."

"Your rounds take you to the Bird Cage?"

"More than once," the lawman said. "That's the town's hot spot for trouble, especially when the miners come in."

"Well, Chapman went back there."

"Thanks for the warnin'."

Clint waved as the sheriff walked away. His own beer was still half full. He decided to sit there and finish it in a leisurely fashion. While he did so he looked around. There was a poker game or two going on at the Bird Cage, but they were small stakes. The games here looked more his style, where a man could lose a lot of money or win a lot. In the morning he'd have to get directions up to Red Mountain Town, so he had the rest of today to kill.

Lindy came over when she saw that the level of his glass was dangerously low.

"Another?"

"No, thanks."

"Still wanna pay for that one? Or are you friends with the sheriff?" she asked, playfully.

"What do I get for being an acquaintance?"

"I guess I can let you slide this one time."

"Those poker games open to anybody?"

"Anybody with money, I guess."

"Thanks, Lindy," he said. "I think I'll play a while."

"Funny," she said, giving him one last shove with her rounded hip, "that was what I had in mind, too."

TEN

Derrick Kyle stared at Arvard Turner, who stood forlornly in front of him in his hotel room.

"I can't believe it," Kyle said. "I told you to make sure the miner didn't meet with Clint Adams."

"I did that!"

"I didn't tell you to kill him!" Kyle shouted. "And I sure as hell didn't tell you to shoot an unarmed man."

"Well, it's done," Arvard said, "and now Sheriff Buckles is lookin' for me—and so is Dan Chapman."

"What do you want me to do about it?" Kyle asked.

"I gotta get out of town!" Arvard cried, plaintively. "I need some money."

"I paid you."

"Not enough."

"I paid you for what I wanted you to do," Kyle said. "I'm not paying you for killing Hangnil."

"You tol' me to do a job," Arvard said. "You didn't tell me how to do it."

"Well," Kyle said, "I guess I didn't realize what an idiot you really are."

Arvard's hand hovered menacingly above his gun. "You can't talk to me that way!"

"Go ahead," Kyle said. He pushed back his jacket to reveal the gun on his hip. "Go for it. Let's see how good you are against someone who's armed."

For a moment it looked as if Arvard Turner would do just that. His body was vibrating with anger. In the end, though, he moved his hand away from his gun.

"I'm just askin' for what's fair," he muttered.

"I'll tell you what's fair," Kyle said. "Me letting you walk out of here alive. I could kill you where you stand and the sheriff would thank me."

"Damn it, Kyle—"

"I tell you what," Kyle said, suddenly struck by an idea. "There's a way you can earn enough money to get away from here."

"How?" Arvard asked, eyeing Kyle suspiciously.

"By making sure the Gunsmith doesn't make it to Red Mountain Town."

Arvard's eyes bugged out.

"How am I supposed to do that?"

"You fancy you know how to use that gun," Kyle said. "Well, go ahead and use it."

"I ain't about to face up to the Gunsmith for no measly two hundred dollars!" That had been the amount he'd been paid to make sure Hangnil didn't meet up with the Gunsmith.

"I'm not talking about two hundred dollars, Arvard," Derrick Kyle said. "I'm talking about a thousand."

"A thousand dollars?"

"That's right."

"But—"

"That's the only way, Arvard," Kyle said. "If you don't get it done, then don't come near me again. Don't come to Red Mountain Town. If you do, I'll either have you killed or I'll do it myself."

For a moment it looked as if the younger man might burst into tears. He backed to the hotel door and reached for the doorknob blindly.

"This ain't fair!" he complained. "You ain't heard the last of me."

"For your sake," Kyle said, "I hope I have, Arvard. That is, unless you come to me and tell me you've killed the Gunsmith."

The young man glared at him and left. Only then did Kyle let his jacket fall down over his holstered Colt.

He walked to the window so he could watch Arvard walk away, but the man must have taken the back stairs. Kyle was not staying in the Beaumont, or in one of Ouray's other fine hotels. He'd chosen to stay in a fleabag at the end of town so no one would notice him. Now he had to get out of town without being seen, as well.

He'd reamed Arvard for killing the miner. Now he was going to have to go back to Red Mountain Town and face his own boss with the news. Nobody had wanted any killing, but now they had it, and they were going to have to cover it up. Maybe he should have dropped Arvard where he stood, but to be frank he wasn't sure he could have taken the boy. Luckily, Arvard was too scared and inexperienced to face another man with a gun. The only way Arvard would be able to handle the Gunsmith was with some help. Or maybe he'd backshoot Clint Adams. Kyle didn't really care. He just didn't want the Gunsmith making his way up to Red Mountain Town. And if Arvard didn't kill Adams and got killed instead—well, that took care of another problem, didn't it?

He looked around the room. He'd only come to Ouray for one day, so he had no baggage. He was leaving nothing behind to betray the fact that he'd been in town. He hadn't even signed the register; he'd just paid the greedy clerk.

Leaving the hotel room, he pulled the door shut and then walked to the back stairs himself. He realized he'd left his horse out there. If Arvard had taken it he'd hunt him down and kill him for sure, or he'd have somebody do it for him.

When he got out back and found his horse was still there, he was relieved. He would have felt foolish if he had to hunt Arvard down after letting him walk out of his room.

He mounted up and headed out of town, wondering if they'd even succeeded in keeping the Gunsmith from finding his way to Red Mountain Town.

ELEVEN

Clint made bigger money in the poker game at Carrie's Place than he had made at the Bird Cage. The stakes were higher, and the players were better. It appeared to be an oddity, though, that better players were easier to beat because they were readable. A bad player will stay in every hand until the end and you have no idea what they have. One bad player in a game of good ones will ruin the entire game.

Clint managed to sit down at Carrie's Place with four pretty good players. During the hands where he folded early he was able to sit back and observe the room, or have a conversation with Lindy when she came over to bring him another coffee. Surprisingly, the coffee at Carrie's was excellent, strong and black, the way he liked it.

He still intended to head to Red Mountain Town in the morning. What he was wondering was whether or not he would need a guide. The men he was playing cards with were not miners, but merchants from town. For that reason none of them had ever been to Red Mountain Town and could not help him.

He was discussing this with them at a time when Lindy brought him a coffee. She stayed to listen, then spoke up.

"I know somebody who can help you, Clint."

He looked up at her. She had the biggest, clearest blue eyes he'd ever seen, and the fact that they were on such a pretty face just intensified their effect.

"Who's that?"

"My brother, Earl," she said. "He goes up there all the time."

"That's right," Ben Morley said. He owned the general store. "He makes deliveries up there for me from time to time. He knows the way pretty well."

Clint looked from Morley back to Lindy.

"Is he in town now?"

"Sure is," she said. "I can have him over here in a few minutes, if ya wanna talk to him."

"A warning, Clint," Morley said. "You'll have to pay the boy."

Boy, Clint thought. Lindy looked to be about twenty-five.

"Younger brother?" he asked her.

"Yeah," she sad. "Earl's twenty-two."

"Paying him won't be a problem," Clint said. "Sure, get him over here. I'll talk to him."

"Okay," she said. "He'll be over here in a jiffy."

"A jiffy's plenty of time for another hand, gents," Tom Baker, the town furrier, said. He finished shuffling the cards and said, "Comin' out."

It became apparent early on to Clint that he was sitting in on a nightly game. It was no wonder these men knew the game, then, playing every night. They also knew each other. What was working in his favor was that they didn't know him. At least, not for the first hour or so.

"It's usually us four," Baker had said, "and then one or two fellas like you, who want to sit in."

So having a stranger in the game was not new to them.

"We can usually tell in the first hour whether or not a fella can play," Morley said.

"Or if he cheats," Les Williams, owner of the hardware store, said.

"You can do the first, and you ain't been doin' the second," the fourth man said. Ted Dekker was the owner of one of the smaller hotels in town. All four men were in their late forties and had settled in Ouray over ten years earlier. They hadn't known each other at all before, but since then had become the closest of friends.

"And if a fella does cheat," Dekker said, "he's pretty sorry about it soon enough."

Since Clint didn't cheat—and had never cheated in his life—he didn't have to worry about what that statement meant.

They actually had time for more than one hand before Lindy approached the table with a young fellow in tow.

"Clint, this is my brother, Earl," she said, proudly.

Earl was tall and thin and looked frightened out of his mind. Obviously, Lindy had told him Clint's name, and he'd recognized it.

"S-sir," Earl said. "P-pleased ta meet ya."

"Earl," Clint said, "why don't we go to the bar, get a beer and have a talk?" He was trying to put the boy at ease.

"Y-yes, sir," Earl replied. "Anything you say."

"Gents," Clint said, "deal me out a few hands."

Clint stood up and put his hand on Earl's shoulder. He felt the young man flinch.

"Relax, Earl," he said, guiding him to the bar. "We're just going to talk and see if I want to hire you as a guide."

"T-that's what Lindy tol' me, sir," Earl said.

"So just relax," Clint said again as they reached the bar. "Bartender, give my friend Earl a beer, and I'll have one, too."

The bartender glared at Earl and asked, "You ain't gonna cause no trouble, are ya, Earl?"

"No, I ain't."

"Boy's a bit of a hothead," the bartender warned Clint.

"That so?"

"When it comes to his sister, yeah," the barman said. "He's a little overprotective, ya might say."

"Well, let us have a couple of beers," Clint said. "There won't be any trouble tonight."

The bartender rolled his eyes and went to get the beers.

TWELVE

Over a beer Clint got Earl to calm down a bit about meeting the Gunsmith. He even got the younger man to agree to call him by his first name.

"What do you need me to do, Clint?" Earl asked.

"I need a guide," Clint told him. "I need to get up to Red Mountain Town."

"I can tell you how to get there," Earl said. "You don't have to pay me to guide you. There's a trail, of a sort."

"I think I might need a little more than a guide," Clint said. "The merchants at the poker table told me that you've worked for them from time to time."

"Yes, sir."

"Have you done any work for anyone on the other end?"

"You mean in Red Mountain?"

"That's what I mean."

"Yes, sir, I have."

"Have you done any work for the two big mining companies? What are they called?" Clint knew, but he wanted to see if Earl knew.

"You mean Reddick or Augustus?"

"Oh, right."

"Well, I've done some work for both, but nothing important. I pretty much just bring things up and down the mountain."

"You mean like a courier?"

"No, sir," Earl said. "I'm more like a delivery man."

"Do you spend much time in Red Mountain Town?"

"Some."

"Know pretty much what's going on there?"

Earl fidgeted a bit.

"You mean like . . . gossip?"

"No, I mean like what's really going on."

"I guess I could tell you what I know."

"Well, since I don't know anything," Clint said, "that would be helpful. If you're willing, Earl, I'd like to hire you to take me up there tomorrow morning."

"That suits me, sir."

"Eight A.M.?" Clint asked.

"That's fine," Earl said. "I'm usually up by six."

"Eight should be good enough—unless it takes half a day to get there?"

"A few hours is more like it."

"Good," Clint said. "Do you have a horse?"

"Yes, sir."

"Then let's meet in front of the Beaumont Hotel at eight."

That impressed Earl.

"You stayin' in the Beaumont?"

"Yes, I am."

"I ain't never been in any of the rooms there."

"Maybe when we get back I'll let you have a look at mine. Not tomorrow, though, because we'll be meeting out front."

"Yes, sir."

"Okay then," Clint said. "Finish your beer. I'm going to go back to the game for a bit before I turn in. Give those fellas a chance to get their money back."

"You're beatin' those fellas?"

"I'm ahead at the moment," Clint said. "We'll have to see how I end up."

Clint could see that Earl was impressed by this, as well. He only hoped that the young man would not be too impressed and tongue-tied to be helpful.

As he was walking back to the table Lindy came up alongside him and asked, "Well?"

"Well, what?"

"Did you hire Earl?"

"I did," Clint said. "He's going to meet me in the morning and guide me up the mountain."

"You're leavin' in the mornin'?"

"That's right."

"That doesn't give us very much time."

"Time for what?" he asked.

"To get better acquainted," she said. "Where are you stayin'?"

"The Beaumont."

"Really?" she said, her eyes widening. "I've never been in any of those rooms."

"Then I should show you mine."

"Yes," she said. "You should. If it's all right with you, I'll come by after work."

"It's fine with me, Lindy."

"I get off late, though," she warned him. "I have to stay until we close."

"I won't be staying here until closing," he said, "but I'll be awake. Just come and knock on the door."

She squeezed his arm and said, "I'll be there."

He watched her walk away, then turned and headed back to the game. Just a few hands, he thought, and then he'd go back to his hotel. He had the feeling he was going to need to get some rest before Lindy appeared at his door.

THIRTEEN

Clint actually did fall asleep in his room while waiting for Lindy to arrive. Luckily, he woke up in time to douse his face and chest with water before her knock came at the door. He opened the door and she slipped in quickly.

"I'm late," she said, removing a shawl she had thrown over her bare shoulders. Her skin almost glowed from the light of the lamp on the wall. "The desk clerk wouldn't let me in."

"How did you get in then?"

"He was going home soon."

"How did you know that?"

She reached behind her to undo her dress. When the top fell away her breasts gleamed in the light. They were full, with heavy undersides and taut, pink nipples.

"I know the schedule of most of the desk clerks in town," she said. "They come into Carrie's and talk."

"So the new clerk let you up?"

"Yes," she said, sliding her dress down over her hips so that it fell to the floor, pooling around her ankles. "He knew me from Carrie's, and he's always had a crush on me."

"A young man, I presume?"

"Very young," she said. "Very inexperienced."

He didn't bother to ask her how she knew that.

She stepped out of her dress, kicked it into a corner and then removed her underwear. Now the light from the lamp shone on the patch of hair between her legs, which looked like spun gold. She was completely naked and her skin was so pale there was almost an aura about her caused by the yellow light.

"Are you finding me just a tad bit forward?" she asked, cocking her head to one side.

He laughed.

"I'm finding you both delightful and beautiful, Lindy."

"Well," she said, bringing her hands up to cup her own breasts from underneath, "with you leavin' in the mornin' we don't have a lot of time, do we?"

"No," he said, "we don't."

His mouth was dry as he watched her rub her thumb over her nipples.

"Then what are you waitin' for?" she asked. "I'm already burnin' for you, Clint Adams. The least you could do is not make a lady wait and get out of your clothes."

She didn't have to ask him twice. He shucked his clothes while she waited impatiently. He could feel the heat her body was giving off from across the room.

He closed the distance between them and ran his hands over the curves of her body. She closed her eyes and moaned, just stood there while he explored her with his hands. Her breasts were heavy when he allowed them to settle into his palms, and when it was his thumbs that brushed her nipples instead of her own she smiled and bit her lip, almost but not quite holding back a growl of pleasure.

"You're hot," he said. "You're skin is burning my hands."

"That's not all I'm gonna burn," she told him. She reached between them and took his fully erect penis in both hands. If he didn't feel the heat of her hands it was only because his pulsing erection was just as hot. She used one hand to stroke him and slid her other down to cup his testicles in her palm, scraping them with her nails.

They stood like that for a few minutes, getting to know each other with their hands until he finally leaned over and touched his lips to her silky skin. He kissed her shoulders, her neck, the upper slopes of her breasts before she pushed him away.

"If you touch my nipples with your mouth I'll go crazy," she warned him. "I'm not ready to go crazy yet."

"I am."

She smiled, her eyes heavy lidded, and said, "Let me see what I can do about that."

FOURTEEN

Arvard had long ago picked out Clint Adams's hotel room window. He stood across the street in the shadows, not wanting to show his face because he knew the sheriff was trying to find him. From the shadows in the window he knew there were two people in the room. He should have moved sooner, but he'd been too cautious, waiting for Clint to fall asleep. Now the Gunsmith had someone with him—a woman, obviously—and his chance to burst into the room and surprise the man was gone. He didn't mind killing a miner, or the Gunsmith, but he knew he'd be hunted to the ends of the earth if he killed an innocent woman.

Seeing no point in waiting longer, he decided that Clint Adams would get to live at least another day. For now, he had to find someplace safe to spend the night.

● ● ●

When Derrick Kyle got back to Red Mountain Town he put his horse up in the livery and walked to his cabin. Red Mountain was far different from Ouray. Here most of the structures were either rickety wood cabins or tents. Ouray had started out this way, but had grown by leaps and bounds, and when the railroad came through recently, the town had hit its stride.

That would never happen to Red Mountain Town because it was too high up. The town—more of a mining camp than anything else—would hardly grow beyond this point. This, however, was where the mines were, where the men worked. In their off time they went down to Ouray, which was the hub of all the small towns and mining camps in the area.

It was quiet as Derrick approached his shack, and a light was burning warmly from inside. The thing of it was, he had not left a light burning. That left only two possibilities. For one he'd need his gun, and for the other he wouldn't. Not knowing which possibility it was, and not willing to take a chance, he drew his gun as he approached his door. When he slammed the door open and darted into the room, gun held ahead of him, the woman on his bed yelped and stared at him with wide eyes.

"Derrick!" she snapped. "You frightened the life out of me."

"Gloria." He holstered his gun, reached behind him and closed the door, sliding the two-by-four into place to lock it.

"What are you doing here?" he demanded.

"What does it look like?" she asked. She was underneath his sheet, which had molded itself to her body, making it clear she was naked. She was slender, with small breasts and butt, but she had a face that could only be described as wanton. From the first moment they'd met they had both felt something between them, and it had not taken them long to act on their urges. "Waiting for you."

"What about your husband?" he asked. "It's late, and he's going to be wondering where you are."

"He's already passed out drunk," she said. "He won't even stir until morning."

"What if someone saw you coming here?"

"No one saw me, Derrick," she promised. "Haven't we gotten good at this?"

It was true, they had gotten used to sneaking around and stealing time together.

He took off his gun belt, laid it aside and removed his jacket.

"Where have you been?" she asked.

"Ouray."

Her eyes flashed.

"You went to town without me?"

"I was in and out quickly," he said. "Had some business to attend to."

"Whose business?"

"Mine," he said.

"And how did it go?"

"Not well."

"Was this really your business . . . or ours?"

He looked at her and felt his heartbeat quickening, his penis thickening. It happened when he saw her dressed, so the way she was sitting now, with the sheet held up just in front of her breasts and her black hair cascading around her shoulders, was twice as exciting. He didn't want her to know, however, just how exciting he found her. He had to maintain control of this relationship. He'd seen too many men lose their heads over a woman and, consequently, everything else, as well. He swore it would not happen to him.

"It was just something I had to take care of."

"But it's not taken care of."

"Don't worry about it," he said. He removed his shirt, and then his boots and trousers. "Have you eaten?"

"Yes," she said.

"I haven't."

"I brought you something," she said. "It's there on the table, covered to keep it warm."

"That was thoughtful," he said. "Thank you."

"But you can't have it, yet," she said, with a smile. "Not until you satisfy me."

With that she dropped the sheet to show him her breasts. Her nipples were brown, her breasts small, but firm, like two ripe peaches.

"Do you think you can do that, Derrick?"

His voice husky with desire, he approached the bed and said, "I think I can give it a good try."

FIFTEEN

True to her word, Lindy did things to Clint that made him crazy. He tried in earnest—and succeeded—in returning the favor.

She began by falling to her knees, taking his hardness into her hands and mouth and making love to it. Clint had had women do this to him before, but many of them simply kissed him or fondled him, sucked him, but this woman . . . she made love to that part of him.

When he couldn't stand it any more—it was too damn good—he reached down, grabbed her beneath her arms and lifted her to her feet. Her eyes were impossibly large, surely big enough to fall into. Her lips were full and he kissed them. She returned his kiss avidly, pressing her body to his. He could feel her firm breasts against his chest, her nipples scratching his chest, like small pebbles. Her tongue blossomed in his mouth and he suckled it for a short time before using his own to press both back into her mouth. They kissed wetly, the sound filling the room. Meanwhile, hands still roamed—his found her firm bottom and cupped it, while she scratched at his back with her nails.

Pressed together they moved across the room to the bed and fell upon it. She seemed more eager—or desperate—than he was so when she fought to be on top, he gave in to her. As she sat atop him, he could feel that she was wet already. She reached between them to take hold of him, held him and slid down on him, taking him inside as easily as a hot knife through butter.

She sighed contentedly as she took him inside, settling fully down on him. He reached up to palm her breasts again, using his thumbs on her nipples. She began to move on him, sliding up and down slowly, her eyes closed, a small smile on her face.

"Oh, my," she said, "that's so nice. You fit just right."

"Thank you, ma'am."

He reached up to take her by the shoulders and bring her breasts down to his lips. He kissed the smooth skin, flicked at the nipples with his tongue, then alternately bit and licked them while she moaned and writhed on him.

Gradually, she began to move on him with more urgency. She sat up straight, pressed her hands down flat on him while rising and falling faster and faster. Her breathing became labored as a flush suffused her body, giving her a rosy glow. He knew she was getting close to her release, but he was far from his, so he let her control the tempo and watched, in fascination, as she worked her way to her climax.

Lindy bit her lip, moaned, made throaty, growling sounds, began to grind herself down onto him. It felt as if her insides were gripping him, then releasing him, as if she had amazing control over those muscles.

It was going to be a long night.

Derrick Kyle peeled back the sheet and tossed it away, revealing Gloria's naked body in all its pale glory. The dark patch between her legs was like a jungle, as black as the hair on her head. He moved to the bed as she came up onto her knees to meet him. She began to pull at his clothes, impatient to have him as naked as she was. When they'd achieved that, he crawled onto the bed with her and began to explore her with his hands and his mouth. Her flesh was hot, almost scalding. He'd never known a woman before whose skin was that hot. Maybe it was because she was married to someone else. Maybe that made her forbidden and, therefore, hot. He'd thought about that in the past, when he was alone in his bed, but now that she was there with him he didn't think about it. In fact, he didn't think at all. He simply enjoyed her.

"Oh, yeah," she groaned as his hand closed over her pubic mound, "this is what I've been waiting for."

She was wet there. He could feel it on his palm, and then on his fingertips as he first stroked her, then probed. She gasped as his fingers entered her, and his mouth captured a nipple at the same time. It always thrilled him, how sensitive she was to his touch. But as much as it thrilled him, it thrilled her more. Her husband was an oaf, and his touch only disgusted her. His fingers were big and blocky, and when he touched her it was for his own pleasure, not hers. And he invariably hurt her. He usually inflicted bruises on her and left her nipples sore. She couldn't wait to get away from him, and she was sore for a long time after being with him. On the other hand, Kyle's fingers were slender and long, and when he touched her, it was to bring her pleasure first. After leaving his bed, she always wanted more. For hours, she would imagine she could still feel his fingers, and his lips, on her.

Now she simply laid back and enjoyed him, tried not to think about what she had to do when they were done here, how she had to go back to her husband.

If only he were dead . . .

Derrick knew that Gloria was ready to be taken, but she'd risked a lot coming there to his cabin and while he was enjoying himself—and her—he decided to punish her.

"Come on," she breathed into his ear, "come on, already . . ."

But instead of entering her he got up onto his knees and stared down at her.

"Turn over," he said.

"Derrick," she replied, warningly, "you know I don't like—"

"Too bad," he said, gruffly.

He took her by the hips and turned her over, then slapped her ass so that she lifted it up.

"Uhn," she grunted as he slid his rigid penis between her thighs and entered her.

He got comfortable, then gripped her hips and began driving in and out of her. Her cries of pleasure were an indication of just how much she actually didn't like it this way . . .

Clint had his cock buried deep inside of Lindy. He had his hands on her thighs, her legs straight up in the air and she was urging him on.

"Deeper," she said, "come on, I want it all."

She had reclined on her back and spread her legs for him, but she hadn't just opened them. She had taken hold of her own ankles and spread them wide. Her hair was so fine down there it was almost as if she didn't have any. He could see right through her thatch to her glistening, pink pussy lips. He had not hesitated at all. If that was what she wanted, then that was what he intended to give her. He'd gotten to his knees between her spreads legs and driven himself home. He couldn't imagine that she could keep her legs open like that, so he slid his hands beneath her thighs to help her. Once he did that she released her own ankles and pressed her hands down on the bed, first flat, and then filling them with the sheet. Soon the air in the room was filled with their grunts and the sounds of their flesh slapping together, and the air became pungent with the smell of sex. Clint could feel his climax building and he fought to hold it down. He didn't want this to end yet, and neither did she. It soon became clear that it would become a test of wills between them as to who would be pushed over the edge first. As Clint stared down at Lindy's face her eyes flared and bored into his. Her nostrils flared and she bit her lip, and he could see the color rising in her face.

It went like that for what seemed hours. Finally, he released one of her ankles and slipped his hand between them. He found her wetness and slid his thumb down until he found her swollen nub. As he touched it she suddenly began to buck beneath him and at that moment he released the stranglehold he had on himself. He exploded inside of her and their movements became so violent that the bed began to hop up and down noisily . . .

SIXTEEN

The next morning Clint rose and tried to leave without waking Lindy but she stirred before he could exit the room.

"What time is it?" she asked.

"Way too early for an honest working girl like you to get up," Clint said. "I've got to meet your brother outside."

"Oh, right," she said, brushing her hair out of her eyes. "That's right. He's guiding you today."

"Yes. Lindy, is there anything I should know about Earl before I leave?"

"Know? Like what?"

"I don't know," Clint said. "Can he use a gun?"

"He can fire a gun."

"Anyone can fire a gun," Clint said. "Can he hit what he aims at?"

"I don't honestly know." She sat up, held the sheet up to her neck. "Is that important?"

"I'm going to be riding in the mountains with a man I don't know," Clint said. "Anything I can find out about him is important."

"Well . . ."

"Is he honest?"

"Well, I . . ."

"Will he try to rob me?"

"Oh, no," she said.

"But he's not completely honest?"

"Well . . . who's completely honest?"

"All right," he said. "I've got to go."

"Will you be back?"

"I suspect I will," he said. "I have to come back through here to get back down the mountain, don't I?"

"I don't know," she said. "I guess so. I don't know if there's a pass or something. . . . Earl would know."

"Okay, then," he said. "I'll keep this room, so stay here as long as you like."

"Thank you, I will."

He didn't kiss her good-bye. It didn't seem appropriate. He wasn't a man leaving his wife in the morning to go to work. He wouldn't be returning that night for supper.

His last sight of her was when she reached up to brush her hair back and the sheet fell away, revealing her big, solid, pale breasts.

Yeah, he thought walking down the hall, he'd be back at least one more time.

When Clint stepped out onto the street, Earl was nowhere to be found, but that was okay. He still had time to go to the livery, saddle Eclipse and walk him back here before the boy was due to meet him. He was surprised, however, when he got the livery and found Earl there, saddling his horse.

"You're early," he said.

Earl turned quickly, startled by Clint's appearance.

"Oh, yeah, I didn't think I ought'ta keep ya waitin'," the younger man said.

"I appreciate that, Earl. I'll saddle my horse and be right with you then."

"Yes, sir."

Clint saddled Eclipse and walked him outside, where he found the boy waiting with a bay mare. She looked to be about seven or eight, solidly built.

"Nice horse," Clint said.

"She's okay," Earl said, patting the mare's nose. "She gets me there and back."

Clint noticed a Winchester rifle on the boy's saddle, but no holster or handgun.

"Can you use that rifle, Earl?"

"Yes, sir," Earl said.

"Ever used it on a man?"

"No, sir," Early said. "Rabbits mostly, and I killed a wolf, once."

"How many shots did it take you to kill the wolf?"

"One."

"And the rabbit?"

"One or two, mostly."

"No handgun?"

"No, sir," Earl said. "I'm no good with a pistol."

"Okay, then," Clint said. "Let's mount up. We need any supplies from the general store?"

"No, sir," Earl said. "We'll be up there before noon."

"That's good," Clint said. "Along the way maybe you can fill me in on a thing or two."

They mounted up and Earl asked, "Like what, sir?"

"Stop calling me *sir*," Clint said. "Just call me Clint."

"Yes, si—uh, all right, Clint. What kinda things do ya want me to tell you?"

"Why don't we just get started?" Clint suggested. "As we ride I'll ask some questions and you answer them if you can. That sound fair?"

"Fair enough, I guess . . . Clint," Earl said.

"Let's get movin', then."

SEVENTEEN

When Derrick Kyle woke the next day Gloria was long gone, but her scent was still present on his sheets and on his own body. Damn it, he thought, he was going to have to take a bath. Couldn't let Gloria's husband—his boss—smell her on him. All that would do was get him fired, and he wasn't willing to risk that, not even for Gloria.

He got dressed and walked into town to the barber shop, which had a bathhouse behind it.

"Got hot water, Fred?" he asked the barber, Fred Harrington.

"I can heat it up for ya," Harrington said, getting out of his own barber chair. There wasn't much call for a barber—or for a bath, for that matter—in a mining town. At least, not until the weekend. Sometimes the miners got spruced up to go down to Ouray, and sometimes they waited until they got there to do it.

Usually it was the ones who were going to be with the whores in Ouray, but then some of them didn't bother. Harrington felt sorry for the whores who had to lie with the unbathed miners.

"Not much call for hot water lately," Harrington said to Kyle. "What brings you in?"

Kyle almost told him it was none of his business, but decided against it.

"I'm starting to smell like a goat, is all."

"Got yerself a gal, Derrick?" Harrington asked. He was an ugly man, tall and thin, in his fifties; these days, he only had a woman if he paid for her. Not that he was much of a ladies man when he was younger, either. Did have a wife once, but that didn't last . . .

"Just get the water, Fred, will you?" Kyle snapped. "I've got to get to work."

"Okay, okay," Harrington said. "Jeez, ya don't gotta yell at me, bite my damn head off, for Chrissake . . ."

He was still muttering as he went back to heat the water.

Kyle was going to have to report to his boss about what had happened in Ouray. He wasn't looking forward to that. He was going to be careful to put the blame squarely on the shoulders of Arvard Turner, but that didn't mean he wouldn't end up getting fired.

He walked to the window and stared out at the muddy street. There was still plenty of gold to come out of the mine, but he wasn't the one who was going to profit from it. Not unless his boss died and he ended up with Gloria. That was a thought that had come to him more than once in the past weeks, not only on his own but from Gloria, too. She made no bones about the fact that she'd like to see her husband dead. She had been very clear on the subject one night . . .

"If he was dead," she'd said one night, after they had finished making love, "I'd have the mine, and you could have me, Derrick."

"Have you?"

"Marry me," she said. "Then the mine—and the gold—would belong to both of us."

He'd thought about that for a few moments. He didn't mind having her in his bed, but did he want to be married to her? After all, wasn't she cheating on the husband she already had? And asking her lover to kill him? What would stop her from doing it again?

"I'd have to think about that, Gloria," he said. "I'd have to think about that long and hard."

"You do that, Derrick," she'd said, sliding her hand down beneath the sheet to take hold of him. "You do that."

And he had. He'd been thinking it over very hard, but he hadn't come to a decision yet. All he knew was that he wasn't ready to get fired.

"Derrick? Water's hot," Harrington said behind him.

"Hot water," he said, turning to follow Harrington. Actually, he'd been in hot water from the moment he started sleeping with his boss's wife. The question now was, could he stand it any hotter?

EIGHTEEN

During the ride up the mountain from Ouray to Red Mountain Town, Clint got to know Earl a little better. He tried to put the boy at ease so he wouldn't constantly be nervous around the Gunsmith. He also thought if he put Earl at ease, he might talk more freely about what went on in Red Mountain.

There was a road from Ouray that went about halfway up the mountain, Earl said, and then petered out.

"What about wagons?"

"Yeah, I've taken a wagon up there a time or two, but it ain't easy goin' with a buckboard."

"Is there another way up?"

"I know some men who have come up from the other side," he said, "but I ain't never been that way. This is the only way I been."

"Well, if you've taken a buckboard up there, it shouldn't be difficult for the horses."

"It ain't," Earl said, "but there is a shortcut we could take, shave some time off the ride."

"Are we in a hurry, Earl?"

"Well, I didn't know if you was."

Clint thought a moment, then said, "I'm not really sure if I am. You see, I don't know who or what's waiting for me in Red Mountain."

"Shortcut, then?"

"Sure," Clint decided, "let's take the shortcut."

When Derrick Kyle entered the mine office, his boss, Jerrod Augustus, glared up at him from behind his desk.

"You seen Gloria today?"

"What?"

"My wife," Augustus said. "You do know my wife, don't you, Derrick?"

"Well, yeah, of course."

"Well, have you seen her this morning?"

"No," Derrick said, "no, I haven't."

"Shit," Augustus said, "probably out spending my money."

Augustus, in his late fifties, was an Easterner who had come West for the gold strike. Proving that it takes money to make money, he had come with backing, enough cash to start a proper mining operation. It was a toss-up each day as to who was taking more gold out of the mountain, Augustus or the Reddick operation.

"Well, where've you been, then?"

"Went down to Ouray, like you told me."

"Anybody see you?"

"No."

"You take care of that little matter we discussed?"

"Uh, well . . ."

"You fucked it up, didn't you?"

"No, not me."

Augustus sat back, the wooden chair creaking beneath his considerable bulk. A bull of a man, he had steel gray hair and lines in his face that looked as if they had been chiseled there.

"Tell me."

Kyle told Augustus what had happened in Ouray, and how it was Arvard Turner's fault. He made that very clear.

"I never told him to kill that miner," he said. "I just told him to make sure he didn't meet up with Adams."

"Idiot."

"Yes, he is."

"No, not him," Augustus said. "You."

"Me? But I didn't—"

"Didn't hire the right man, that's what you didn't do," Augustus said. "And maybe I didn't, either, when I hired you to be my foreman."

"No, Jerrod—"

"Adams on his way up here?"

"Maybe."

"Where's Turner?"

"Still out there."

Augustus rubbed his hand over his jaw, the stubble making scratching noises on his rough palm.

"We'll just have to wait and see, then, if Adams makes it, we'll take it from there."

"Okay. Whataya want me to do in the mean—"

"Get up to the mine and see that everything is running properly. That's your real job, ain't it?"

"Yeah, it is."

"And while you're at it," Augustus called after Kyle as the foreman left the office, "find my wife and tell her I want to see her!"

Taking the short way meant walking the horses over some rocks here and there but both animals seemed up to the task. Eclipse was not much of a mountain climber but he kept up with the mare, who proved to be remarkably surefooted. The way seemed almost effortless until the first shot came. Clint heard the bullet hit meat and bone, saw Earl go down, then dove for cover as a flurry of shots followed.

NINETEEN

Judging from the number of bullets that were winging their way around, there was more than one shooter. Clint took cover behind some rocks, but couldn't see Earl from where he was.

"Earl?" he called when the shots subsided into silence.

No answer.

"Come on, Earl? You there?"

That was all he had to do, get Lindy's brother killed on the first day Earl was working for him.

Then the weak reply came.

"I-I'm here. I'm hit."

"Bad?"

"M-my shoulder."

"Just stay down," Clint said.

But staying down was something he couldn't do. It was cold and getting colder as the day went on. On a warmer day he'd wait out the shooters, make them come to him. But for right now he had to locate them, and the only way to do that was to get them shooting again. And the only way to do that was to stand up.

He drew his gun, wishing he had his rifle; but that was with Eclipse, who had wisely put some space between himself and the shooting. Clint didn't know where the mare had gone, or if she was down.

Gun in hand he stood up quickly and made his way towards Earl. He figured if he was going to get shot at, he might as well find out how the boy was doing. Sure enough a volley of shots came his way, chewing up the dirt in front and behind him, and chipping pieces of the rocks, kicking up sparks at the same time. However, whoever was doing the shooting, they were poor shots and he did not once come close to being hit. Still, the odds were against him the more lead came his way.

He reached the rock he thought Earl was behind and found the boy crouched there, clutching his shoulder. Ribbons of blood had leaked out from between his fingers.

"Hey, kid," he said, holstering his gun. "How you doing?"

"F-fine," Earl said. "H-hurts."

"Yeah, I'll bet. Let me have a look."

He pried the boy's hand away from the wound and examined it. He was afraid the bullet might have struck a bone. There was no exit wound, so it was still in there. If it had gone through and come out the boy's back, Earl would be in worse shape. A bullet's exit wound was always larger than its entrance wound.

"Am I gonna die?" Earl asked.

"No." Clint removed the boy's bandana. "Hold this against the wound. It'll slow the blood flow."

"What're you gonna do?"

"I'm going to get us out of here so I can get you to a doctor," Clint said. "That is, if there's a doctor in Red Mountain."

"Mrs. Augustus is the closest thing," he said. "She can patch bullet wounds. She's done it before."

"Then we'll have to get you to Mrs. Augustus. Just stay low until I come back."

"I—I wish I had a gun."

"What for?" Clint asked. "You told me you can't hit anything, anyway."

"I'd just feel better, is all."

Clint had an extra gun, his .32 Colt New Line, but it was his hideout gun. It would not do any good at a distance, and besides, it was in his saddlebag.

"Sorry, kid," he said. "No gun. Just sit tight."

Clint thought he had the shooters spotted, and his estimation was that there were three of them. Lucky for him they were terrible shots, so he thought he'd be able to work his way closer to them.

He drew his gun again and prepared to stand up. This time, he was going to run straight at them. Maybe that would unnerve them, cause them to run.

After all, it was a crazy thing to do.

Arvard Turner looked down at the rocks Clint Adams had ducked behind.

"I think we hit the other one," Milt Mackler said.

"I don't care about the other one," Arvard said. "Adams is the one we want."

"You sure he's the real Clint Adams?" the other man, Greg Scully, asked. "I mean, the honest-to-God Gunsmith?"

"That's him, all right."

"Jesus," Mackler said, "we'd better not let him get close enough to use that handgun."

"Well, if you fellas would shoot straighter maybe he won't," Arvard said.

"You sure we're gettin' paid good for this, Arvard?" Scully asked. "I mean, we ain't seen any money yet."

"Don't worry," Arvard lied. "Yer getting paid plenty."

"There he is!" Mackler said. "What the hell is he doin'?"

"Just start shootin'!" Arvard hollered.

"He's runnin' right at us," Scully said. "He's crazy!"

"Just shoot," Arvard said, and followed his own order, firing as fast as he could.

TWENTY

Just before he started rushing the shooters Clint wished that Earl did have a handgun. He could have used a gun in each hand. He had taken three steps before the men situated above him started firing. Once again the ground around him was chewed up by lead, but he couldn't be that lucky forever. He started firing, laying down some cover for himself. He made some progress, then found himself some cover again and reloaded.

"Jesus Christ," Arvard swore. "You missed!"

"You missed, too," Mackler said.

They were all reloading.

"Well, he's closer now," Scully said.

"Then you should be able to hit him easier," Arvard told them.

Mackler and Scully noticed that Arvard continued to ignore the fact that he was also firing wildly.

"We never said we was great shots," Scully said. "You needed two men who could shoot. We can shoot."

"You just can't hit anything."

"Neither can you!" Mackler said, frustrated.

"I'm better with a pistol," Arvard told the man. "You wanna see?"

"Yeah," Mackler said, "I wanna see—on him. Let Adams get closer and then show us how good you are."

Arvard almost pulled his pistol and plugged Mackler right there, but he would have had to kill Scully, too.

"Get ready," Scully said, breaking up the argument. "I think he's comin' again."

Clint clutched his reloaded pistol in his right hand, stood and started running again. Immediately, he realized something had changed. There were more guns firing than before and not all of them were firing at him. As he looked ahead of him he saw the three shooters stand, and then one spun and fell, as if hit by a bullet, but not one of his. The other two men started running, and now no one was firing at him. He continued up the slope until he reached the position the three men had been firing from. There were ejected cartridge casings all over the place, and one dead man. When he heard someone approaching from a different angle he turned, his gun ready, but relaxed when he saw who it was.

"You," was all he said.

"I heard the shooting and thought I'd better take a

look," Dan Chapman said. His gun was holstered, presumably after being reloaded.

"Lucky you did," Clint said. "You know this jasper?"

"Lemme take a look."

They both leaned over the dead man so they could see his face.

"No, I never seen him."

"Me, neither," Clint said.

"You hit?" Chapman asked.

"No, but the kid guiding me to Red Mountain Town is. He's down there. I need to get him to a doctor."

"No doctor in Red Mountain, but it's the closest place," Chapman said. "Mrs. Augustus can patch him up, if the wound ain't too serious."

"Don't tell him," Clint said, "but I think the bullet hit bone. It's still in there, so she'll be able to dig it out."

"Won't be able to tell if it hit bone until he tries using that arm," Chapman said.

"You know it and I know it, but I don't want him to know it. That okay with you?"

"No skin off my nose. Who's the kid?"

"Earl . . . Christ, I don't even know his last name." Lindy's either, for that fact, although he assumed they were the same.

"Earl Simms, if it's the young fella I think it is."

"Why don't you fetch your horse and meet me down there," Clint suggested. "We might need you to rustle up our mounts . . . if you don't mind."

"Hell, no," Chapman said. "I'm headed back to Red Mountain Town myself."

Clint hurried back down to where he'd left Earl. The boy was sitting with his back against a rock, gritting his teeth and clutching his shoulder.

"What happened?" he asked.

"We got some help from a fella named Chapman."

"Dan Chapman?" Earl asked. "I know him."

"Says he knows you, too."

"He works for Reddick."

"I knew he was a miner, but I didn't know which outfit he worked for. He's going to gather up our horses and then we'll get you to Red Mountain so you can get patched up."

"Sorry I wasn't much use to you, Mr. Adams."

"You did fine, son," Clint said. "And the name's Clint, remember?"

Chapman rode over to them, trailing both horses behind him. Eclipse hadn't gone too far, but he'd had to ride some to collect the mare.

Together they got Earl up on his horse.

"Reckon you were using this shortcut, too, so I also guess you know the way," Clint said.

"Don't worry," Chapman said. "I'll get us there."

Some miles away Arvard Turner and Milt Mackler reined their horses in.

"You didn't tell us he'd have help!" Mackler said, angrily.

"I didn't know."

"Well, goddamnit, now my partner's dead!"

"Whataya want me to do about it?" Arvard asked. "You knew you was gonna get shot at."

"Yeah," Mackler said, "but for money. I ain't seen no money, kid."

Arvard looked at the older man.

"I told you there'd be money when the job was done."

"Yeah, well, this is one job you're gonna finish by yerself," Mackler said. "I want my money and then I'm outta here."

"I told you, you'll get paid—"

Mackler put his hand on his pistol.

"You think you're so all-fired good with that gun you'd better use it, sonny, or pay me."

"Use it or pay you?" Arvard asked.

"That's right."

The young man shrugged, said, "Your call," then drew and shot the man dead before he could clear leather.

Arvard Turner was very impressed with himself.

TWENTY-ONE

Red Mountain Town was a mud hole.

At least, that's what it looked like to Clint as they rode in. It had started raining on them about a mile out of town, and already the holes and ruts in the street were filled with muddy water.

"So, where do we find this Mrs. Augustus?" Clint asked Dave Chapman.

"At the mine office, I guess. It's this way."

Clint looked over at Earl just as the young man started to slide from his saddle because he had either fallen asleep or had passed out.

"Earl?" Clint slapped the boy's knee.

"Huh? Wha—?"

"We're almost there, son," Clint said. "Stay in the saddle."

"Yes, sir," Earl said. "I'll do my best."

Chapman led them to the far end of town and stopped in front of a wooden structure that bore a sign over the door that proclaimed it to be the office of the Augustus Mining Company.

"I'll see if she's inside," Chapman offered.

"How about I do that?" Clint asked. "You stay with Earl, make sure he doesn't fall out of the saddle."

"Sure thing," Chapman said. "Your call, Adams. Just tiptoe around Augustus. He ain't easy to get along with."

Clint turned and looked at Chapman.

"And you work for Reddick?"

"That's right."

"Foreman?"

"Me? Naw." Chapman shook his head. "The foreman's a fella named Howard, Frank Howard."

"I see. But you know Augustus?"

"Adams," Chapman said, "everybody hereabouts knows both Augustus and Bill Reddick. They're the biggest men in these parts."

"Well," Clint said, "I guess I'll be finding that out for myself, starting with Augustus."

With that he turned and walked to the front door of the mining office. He had the courtesy to knock, but was in too much of a hurry to wait for a reply. He opened the door and entered.

When Jerrod Augustus looked up at the man who had just entered his office he frowned.

"What do you want?"

"I need your wife."

"What?" Augustus's face grew red.

"I've been told your wife is the closest thing to a

doctor around here," Clint said. "I've got a man with a bullet in his shoulder. A boy, really."

"Boy? What boy?"

"His name's Earl Simms."

"Earl? I know that boy." Augustus stood up. He was a barrel-chested man who looked to Clint like he could wrestle a grizzly. "He's a decent sort. Bring him right in here. I'll try to find my wife. There's a cot in that corner."

Augustus pointed, then hurried out the door, leaving a stunned Clint behind. Hard to get along with? The man had leaped at the chance to help Earl.

What was he missing?

Chapman and Clint had gotten the boy situated on the cot when Jerrod Augustus returned with his wife. The tall, willowy brunette was stunning; she brushed past all the men to lean over Earl and examine his wound.

"Which one of you is responsible for this?" she asked, without looking at them.

"Not me," Chapman said.

She turned her head and glared at Clint.

"You, mister? Are you responsible for getting this boy shot?"

"He was helping me when he was shot," Clint said, removing his hat. "I guess maybe that makes me responsible."

"You didn't pull the trigger?" Augustus asked.

"No, sir, I did not," Clint said. "In fact, I was being shot at, same as he was."

"That's right," Chapman said. "When I came along they was pinned down. Adams and me run them off."

"Adams?" Augustus asked.

"That's right," Chapman said, before Clint could say a word. "He's Clint Adams."

Clint saw Augustus react as if he'd been slapped, but Earl spoke before anyone else could.

"It wasn't Mr. Adams's fault, Mrs. Augustus," he said. "Don't blame him."

"You hush now, Earl. Just rest easy." She stood up, looked at the three men and said, "Gentlemen?"

She walked to the other end of the room and they followed.

"The bullet is still in there, and it's deep."

"I think it might have struck bone," Clint said.

"If that's true it may be wedged in," she said. "I'll have to see if I can get it out."

"What do you need, Gloria?" Augustus asked.

"I need plenty of bandages, a basin of hot water and a knife—a sharp one."

"I'll have someone start tearing bandages from a sheet," her husband said. "Chapman, you get the water."

"Yes, sir?"

"And the knife?" she asked.

"I've got one in my saddlebag that will do the trick," Clint said.

"It will need to be sterilized."

"We'll build a fire in the fireplace," Augustus said, pointing to the one in the back wall.

"Then get to it, gents," Gloria said. "This boy does not have all day!"

TWENTY-TWO

Once the water was boiled, the bandages were prepared and the knife was sterilized, Gloria Augustus kicked everyone out of the building except Clint.

"Suits me," Chapman said and left.

Augustus eyed his wife and Clint suspiciously, but Gloria said, "Do you want me to help this boy?"

Augustus allowed as he did, so he left.

"Hold him down," she told Clint. "I'm going for that bullet."

"Wait," Clint said. "He needs something to bite down on or he's going to bite off his tongue."

"A piece of leather."

"Let me get his belt."

"Never mind that," she said. "Give me yours."

He started to unbuckle his gun belt so he could get at his belt and she made a grab for it.

"No," he said. "I need this. Wait." He removed his

96

regular belt and gave it to her. She set it between the boy's teeth.

"Must be a hell of a way to live," she said.

"What do you mean?" he asked, as he put his hands on Earl to hold him down. One hand on his un-injured shoulder, the other on his chest. It brought the two of them into very close proximity, and he could smell her. She smelled fresh enough, but there was something else . . . and then he got it. She smelled like sex. Either she'd had sex recently, or this situation was getting her excited.

"I mean being afraid to be without your gun, even when you're in the room with a woman and an in-jured boy."

"Anyone can pull a trigger, Mrs. Augustus."

"Just call me Gloria," she said, "and hold him steady. If he jerks too hard I could end up killing him."

"I've got him."

She began probing for the bullet. At first Earl screamed and bit down on the belt, then he tried to buck. Clint held him down firmly, and the boy passed out.

"He fainted," she said, "that's good. But continue to hold him down, just in case."

He did. She started to sweat. It popped out on her head and began to stain the dress under her arms. The odor was pungent, and sexy, and now it was he who was getting excited. He wondered if anyone would mind if he threw her down on the floor and took her when she was done.

He didn't think she'd mind, but her husband might.

• • •

Gloria Augustus wondered what was going on? Here she was trying to get a bullet out of poor Earl's shoulder and all she could think about was getting out of her clothes and falling to the floor with Clint Adams. She felt herself blush furiously at the thought and hoped Clint would mistake it for turning red from the effort she was exerting.

Her husband was boring, sand-poor Derrick was simply better than nothing, but in Clint Adams she felt she had found a truly exciting man, even though she'd only met him half an hour before. She was aware of his reputation as the Gunsmith, because when her husband had told her they were going west, she had steeped herself in the lore of the old West. The lore and the lure, and now, here was the lure— Clint Adams.

Using the tip of the knife, she found the bullet. As soon as she touched it, it moved, which meant it wasn't lodged in or against a bone, but that still didn't mean it hadn't hit one. Poor Earl was going to have to wait to heal to find out how much movement he had in that arm.

"I've got it," she said.

"Good girl," Clint said, and it sent chills up and down her spine. How idiotic was she acting?

She pried the bullet free and dropped it into the basin of water. She then proceeded to cleanse the wound, stitch it and bandage it. All of this she managed to get done before Earl came around.

"Wha—"

"Relax, Earl," Clint said. "The bullet's out and you're patched up, thanks to Mrs. Augustus."

"Gloria," she told Clint. "Just call me Gloria."

When Gloria and Clint stepped outside they found Augustus and another man waiting.

"Adams," the mine owner said. "This is my foreman, Derrick Kyle."

"Adams," Kyle said, eyeing both Gloria and him like a jealous husband. Clint immediately felt the tension in the air and wondered if Augustus felt it, too.

"Kyle."

The two men nodded, but did not shake hands.

"How did it go?" Augustus asked his wife.

"He'll be all right. We'll have to move him to the boardinghouse so he can get some rest."

"I'll have a stretcher prepared and have some of the men carry him over." He looked at Clint. "Earl is well-liked around here."

"That's nice." Clint thought the boy wasn't as well-liked down in Ouray.

"Will you be staying around?" Augustus asked.

"Just for a little while," Clint said. "I believe I have some business around here."

"Oh? With whom?"

Augustus, his wife and his foreman seemed very interested in the answer.

"You know?" Clint asked. "I'm not sure."

TWENTY-THREE

Clint helped carry Earl to a nearby rooming house. He made payment arrangements with the middle-aged woman who ran the house and gave her three days in advance. Gloria Augustus had advised him not to try to take Earl down the mountain before then. He also arranged for a room for himself. The woman told him he was lucky; it was her last one. When he checked it out, he found that it wasn't much of a room. Just a cot and four walls, but it was enough. He didn't plan on being there very long.

When he had Earl situated, he came out and found Chapman waiting for him.

"Figured you might have some questions."

"Like who's the law around here?"

"There's no badge-toter up here," Chapman said. "Buckles is the law, and when we need him we send for him."

"And until he gets here?"

"We do the best we can." Chapman said. "That usually means Derrick Kyle or Frank Howard."

"The two foremen?"

Chapman nodded.

"If it's a problem involving an Augustus man, then Kyle upholds the law. If it's a Reddick man, the job falls to Frank."

"And if it falls somewhere in the middle?"

"They work together," Chapman said.

"Do they get along?"

"They're not friends, if that's what you mean. But they manage to work together when they have to."

"Well, I've met Kyle," Clint said. "I suppose I should meet Frank Howard. Maybe he can tell me who sent for me."

"What if nobody steps up?" Chapman asked. "What if nobody admits to sendin' for you?"

"I guess I'd be on my way, then."

"I'll take you to meet Frank," Chapman said. "You should probably meet Mr. Reddick first, though."

"Fine with me," Clint said. "Lead the way."

Clint followed Chapman through the small mining town. The man seemed to know where every mud puddle was.

"Don't walk in that one," the man warned, pointing. "So far we've lost two men, a dog and a horse in there."

When they arrived at the office of the Reddick Mining Company he found much the same thing he'd found at the Augustus mining office—a precarious-looking wood structure with a sign on it. He wondered why, if these two mining companies were taking so much gold out of the mountain, they'd not been able to build sturdier offices.

Chapman opened the door of the mining office and entered without knocking. Clint followed. The similarity between the two offices held up on the inside. A couple of desks, some wooden chairs and pieces of mining materials placed all around. Behind one of the desks sat a man in his late forties who didn't resemble Jerrod Augustus at all. This man was long and lean, with the look of an undertaker rather than a miner. He didn't look like he'd have the strength to do any mining.

"Chapman," the man said. "There you are. What the hell happened to you?"

"Bad news, boss," Chapman said. "Hangnil's dead."

"What?"

Briefly, Chapman told his boss what had happened to Hangnil, then ended by introducing him to Clint.

"Adams?" Bill Reddick said. He stood up and extended his hand. "The Gunsmith?"

"That's right, Mr. Reddick," Clint said. "You wouldn't by any chance have been expecting me, were you?"

"Expecting you?" Reddick frowned. "Why would I have been expecting you?"

"Somebody sent for Clint and he doesn't know who it was," Chapman said. "Hangnil was sent down the mountain to fetch him."

"By whom?"

"We don't know."

"I received an unsigned telegram," Clint said.

"And on the strength of that you came here all the way from . . ." Reddick paused.

"Texas."

"But why?"

"It might have been from a friend in trouble."

"Why wouldn't a friend sign the telegram?" Reddick asked.

"I'm going to ask him that when I find him."

"Well," Reddick said. "It wasn't me. I mean, we don't even know each other."

"Well," Clint said, "maybe you have someone working for you I do know. You or Augustus."

"He didn't send for you, did he?" Reddick asked, suddenly suspicious.

"He says not," Clint answered.

Reddick looked relieved.

"What if he had?" Clint asked.

"Augustus and I have our differences, but neither one of us wants to bring gunfighters into it," Bill Reddick said. "At least, we haven't up until now."

Clint didn't bother explaining that he was not a gunfighter. It wasn't important at the moment.

"Is Frank around, Mr. Reddick?" Chapman asked. "I told Clint I'd introduce him."

"You think my foreman sent for you?" Reddick asked. "Why would he?"

"I'm just hoping he'll know who did."

"Still think you came a long way on the strength of an unsigned telegram."

"Let's just say I had nothing better to do."

"Well, Frank's around here somewhere," Reddick said to Chapman. "Go ahead and introduce them."

"Come on," Chapman said. "Let's take a look outside."

"Uh, before you leave town, Adams," Reddick said as Clint and Chapman reached the door, "stop in again."

"What for?"

Reddick shrugged, "Just a talk."

Clint hesitated, then said, "Sure, Mr. Reddick. It never hurts to talk, does it?"

TWENTY-FOUR

Outside Clint put his hand on Chapman's arm.

"What's going on up here?"

"Whataya mean?"

"Something's eating that man."

Chapman shrugged.

"He doesn't confide in me, Clint," the man said. "I'm just the hired help."

"What do you do up here?" Clint asked.

"I work the mines," Chapman said. "I told you. I've got my own little strike, but I have to work for Reddick to make enough money to work my strike."

"They didn't hire you for your gun?"

"I don't even think they know about that."

"You still wear your gun."

"A lot of people wear a gun," Chapman said. "If Hangnil had been wearin' a gun, maybe he wouldn't be dead."

"I don't think that would make much of a difference," Clint said. "Is there anyplace we can get a drink before we go looking for Frank Howard?"

"Sure," Chapman said. "Come on."

He led Clint to a large tent. Inside, the setup looked remarkably like the inside of a regular saloon. A bar, gaming tables and girls.

"Yep," Chapman said. "They had to lug that bar and the tables up the mountain."

"They?"

"Two partners," Chapman said. "Hal Charles and Danny Worth. They figured they'd do better up here than down in Ouray competing with other saloons."

"They're the only saloon in Red Mountain Town?"

"The only one."

They went to the bar where Chapman greeted the bartender, Lew, by name.

"What'll ya have, Chappy?" Lew asked. He was a large man in his thirties, with shirtsleeves pushed up above huge biceps. Clint knew that in mining operations like this the bartenders sometimes doubled as bouncers.

Chapman looked at Clint.

"Beer cold?" Clint asked.

"As cold as the snow can keep it," Lew said.

"Beer, then."

"Two," Chapman said.

"Comin' up, gents."

It was early evening and the girls were starting to circulate around the room. There were already plenty of miners there, drinking and playing cards, and Clint knew there would be more on the way when they got out of the mines.

"What's on your mind?" Chapman asked.

"What do you mean?"

"You weren't just thirsty," the other man said. "You want to ask me somethin'?"

"We didn't talk much after the shooting," Clint said. "Did you see who the other two men were?"

"All I saw was a big man and a small one. My guess is the small one will turn out to be Arvard Turner."

"Why would Turner be shooting at Earl and me?"

"Not Earl," Chapman said. "You."

"Okay, then, why me?"

"Why Hangnil?" Chapman asked. "To keep him from meetin' up with you. But you head up here anyway, so I figure he was tryin' to stop you from gettin' here."

"To find the man who sent for me," Clint said.

Chapman nodded and sipped his beer.

"If it's not one of the mining owners," Clint asked, "who would it be?"

"I got no idea."

"You can't guess?"

"I do my job, and I work my claim, Clint," Chapman said. "That's all I do. After that I mind my own business."

"What about your friend Hangnil?"

"What about Ben?"

"Didn't he do his job?"

"He did his job, and he did odd jobs," Chapman said. "In that way he's a little like your young friend, Earl."

Clint made wet circles on the bar with his beer mug. Somebody on this mountain had sent for him, and somebody else had to know who that was.

"Okay," he said, finally. "Let's finish these up and find your foreman, find out what he knows."

"And if he doesn't know anything?" Chapman said. "Will that send you on your way?"

"I've been shot at, Chapman, and Earl caught a bullet which was probably meant for me," Clint said. "I'm not leaving this area until I find out what's going on."

"Can't say I blame you for that," Dan Chapman said. "And do me a favor."

"What's that?"

"From now on, just call me Chappy. Everybody does."

TWENTY-FIVE

Clint followed Chappy along the muddy streets after they finished their beers and fended off the advances of a couple of the girls.

"Not as pretty as that Lindy down in Ouray," Chapman said, "but it's hard to get girls who want to work up here."

"Where are we headed?"

"Frank has a shack at the edge of town away from everything," Chapman said. "He spends a lot of time there."

"Not in the saloon?"

"Frank's kinda . . . strange," Chappy said. "He likes to spend time alone. Every once in a while he sends for one of the girls, but that's about it."

"What about food?"

"He's got a small stove. Speaking of that, we're in luck. See? Smoke from his chimney."

It wasn't much of a chimney, just a lead pipe stuck

on the roof, but then it wasn't much of a roof. Chappy had been right, Frank Howard did live in a shack.

Chappy stepped up to the flimsy front door and pounded on it.

"Frank? It's Chappy. Open up!"

A few moments went by and then the door swung inward. The man inside stayed back in the shadows, but Clint could see the six-gun in his hand.

"You don't need that, Frank," Chapman said. "It's just me. I got somebody I want ya to meet."

There was no response from inside right away. Clint could smell cooking meat and suddenly his stomach was growling.

"And we could use somethin' to eat if ya got enough," Chappy added.

There was a tense moment when Clint wondered if he was going to have to draw his gun. Apparently, Frank Howard was not a trusting man. He was probably on the run and took this job under an assumed name. That was why he stayed to himself as much as he could.

Then, suddenly, the man backed up. Chapman turned to Clint and said, "It's okay."

Chappy went in first and then Clint. Frank Howard had moved to the stove and had his back to them. Clint didn't see the gun.

"Smells good, whatever it is," Chappy said.

No reply.

"What's with the gun, Frank?" Chapman asked. "What're you so nervous about?"

"Who's your friend, Chappy?" the man asked with his back still to them.

"His name's Clint Adams," Chapman said.

No reaction.

"You know who he is?"

"I know."

Clint frowned. There was something familiar about the man's voice, but he couldn't quite place it.

"I'm fryin' up some steaks and spuds," Frank Howard said. "That good enough for you fellas?"

"Fine by me," Chapman said.

"Me, too," Clint said.

"Got water or whiskey to drink."

"Whiskey," Chappy said.

"Water," Clint replied.

"Whiskey's in that cupboard behind you, Chappy."

Chappy got up and retrieved a half a bottle of whiskey from a three-legged cupboard and brought it to the table.

"I'll pump us some water after I set these plates down on the table for you boys."

Finally, his hands filled with plates, the man turned and walked to the table. He had a full beard. Clint hadn't seen him in a lot of years, but he found himself looking into the face of Frank James—Jesse James's brother.

TWENTY-SIX

The look in Frank's eye was very clear. He didn't want Clint giving him away.

Chapman poured out three whiskeys, even though Clint had not asked for one. Frank put the plates down on the table. It was clear he'd been cooking two steaks for himself, but he'd divvied them up three ways, along with the potatoes. He went back to the sink and pumped some water for Clint, brought it over in a tin cup, then sat down with Clint and Chapman.

"This is decent on you, Frank," Chapman said.

"You want to fill me in on why you're here while we eat?" Frank "Howard" asked.

"I'll let Clint do that," Chapman said, around a mouthful of meat and potatoes.

Clint, who was now very sure who it was had sent him the telegram, went through the motions of telling Frank Howard his story.

"And you don't know who sent you the telegram?"

Frank asked, going along with the story.

"No, I don't." He was getting tired of being asked that and at the same time was starting to wonder about it himself. Had he been that bored?

Clint Adams and Frank James continued to talk about things that had happened since Clint's arrival in Ouray.

"I know Earl," Frank said, when told that the boy had been shot. "He's a good kid."

"Somebody didn't think so," Clint said.

"Most likely the same fella who killed Ben Hangnil," Chapman said.

"Hangnil's dead?" Frank asked.

"Yes," Clint said. "Apparently, he'd been sent down to fetch me and got killed for it."

"By whom?" Frank asked.

"A man named Arvard Turner," Clint said.

"You know this for a fact?"

"He did it at the saloon in front of a roomful of people," Chapman said. "Yeah, we know it for a fact."

"Damn!" Frank swore.

He fell silent after that and as soon as all three men had finished their food he collected the plates and took them away; only then did he drink the whiskey that Chapman had poured for him. Chapman had drunk two with dinner and had a third before Frank took the bottle from him.

"You got work to do, don't you?" he asked.

"I was just guidin' Clint around—"

"I'll take care of that, Dan," Frank said. "Go back to work."

Chapman hesitated, then said, "Okay, Frank. You're the boss."

Clint and Frank waited until Chapman had left before shaking hands.

"Good to see you, Frank," Clint said.

"It's been a while," Frank said.

"Since Jesse was killed."

Frank nodded.

"I was glad they didn't convict you," Clint said.

"Might have been better if they had."

"Why do you say that?"

Frank shrugged.

"It hasn't been easy tryin' to live as Frank James," he admitted. "Not since Jesse died. Everybody wants to know what really happened, what I'm gonna do about it."

"So you took the name Frank Howard?" Clint asked. Jesse, when he was shot to death, had been living as Thomas Howard.

"It was as good a name as any."

"How'd you end up here?"

"I started takin' odd jobs, got interested in mining. I don't know much beyond bank and train robbin'."

"So now you know enough about mining to become a foreman?" Clint asked.

Frank smiled. "A little bit of knowledge and a lot of fast talkin'."

Frank poured two glasses of whiskey and handed Clint one. Not much of a whiskey drinker, Clint took it, nevertheless.

"To Jesse," he said, lifting his glass.

"To Jesse," Frank said. They drank and set the empty glasses down on the table.

"Now you want to tell me what the hell is going on up here?" Clint asked.

TWENTY-SEVEN

"I've got a good thing going here, Clint."

"I'm glad for you, Frank," Clint said. "That still doesn't explain why you sent me that telegram."

"Have a seat."

They both sat.

"More?" Frank asked, raising the whiskey bottle.

"Not for me."

"I forgot, you don't drink whiskey much, do you?"

"Only for special toasts."

"I won't need a glass, then. Ain't much left, anyway."

There was about an inch left at the bottom of the bottle. Frank upended and finished it. His beard made him look older, closer to fifty than forty. Clint knew that he was somewhere in between.

He waited patiently while Frank killed the bottle and set it down.

"Takes more than that to chase away the demons," Frank said.

"It always does."

"Clint," Frank said, "the two men who own these mines up here are idiots. They're Easterners who don't know what they're doin' here."

"I gathered that."

"You met 'em both?"

Clint nodded. "And Gloria Augustus."

"Her," Frank said. "She's dangerous. Stay away from her. She'll eat you alive."

"I can think of worse ways to go."

"She's already sleepin' with the foreman over there."

"Derrick Kyle?"

Frank nodded.

"Does her husband know?"

"He's a fool if he doesn't," Frank said. "Everybody else knows about it."

"Anybody tell him?"

"Nobody wants to lose their job."

"How'd you come to be working for Reddick?"

Frank shrugged.

"He's the one who hired me first."

"How long you been up here?"

"About four months."

"You don't seem happy."

"Happy died with Jesse, Clint."

"I can understand that, Frank," Clint said, "but you've got to go on living."

"Do I?"

"If you didn't want to, you wouldn't be up here."

"Okay," Frank said. "Let's assume that then. I'm up here because I want to live."

"What's your good thing?" Clint asked. "You getting a good salary?"

"That and a percentage."

"And what do you have to do to get that percentage, Frank?" Clint asked.

"Just make sure that the Reddick operation is number one up here," Frank replied.

"Two gold mines," Clint said, "both doing well, right?"

"Right."

"So what the hell does it matter which one is number one, and which is number two?"

"It matters to these two men."

"And therefore it matters to you."

"If I want to get my percentage, yeah."

"So what's the problem?" Clint asked. "Why do you need me?"

"Because I can't trust anybody else," Frank said. "Jesse was the only man I could ever trust. For a while I thought Cole was somebody I could trust, but it didn't turn out that way. It was only Jesse . . . and now you."

"Why me?"

"Because you always kept your word to us," Frank said. "Jesse said you were the only friend he ever had besides me."

"I'm flattered."

It had been Jesse James who gave Clint his big black gelding, Duke, who had recently been put out to pasture in favor of another black, the Darley Arabian, Eclipse. Clint had never forgotten that.

"Jess was always a good judge of character."

"Now you're laying it on a little thick, Frank," Clint said. "Just tell me what's going on."

Frank hesitated, then said, "Somebody up here knows who I really am."

"And they're blackmailing you?"

Frank nodded.

"Why not just come clean, Frank?"

"Look," Frank replied, "all Reddick and Augustus know about the James boys is what they read in the yellow-backed novels back East. I can't fight that right now."

"What do you want me to do?"

"Watch my back, and find out who it is."

"And then?"

"Get rid of them."

"Frank—"

"Oh, I don't mean kill them, Clint," Frank said, hurriedly. "I mean just what I say—get rid of them!"

TWENTY-EIGHT

"What's in it for me, Frank?" Clint asked.

"You don't think I asked you to come all this way for nothin', do you?" Frank James asked. "I'll cut you in for part of my share."

"Why not take care of it yourself?"

"I'm not Frank James up here, Clint," Frank said. "I'm Frank Howard and I have to stay Frank Howard. I don't even carry a gun around here."

"Any idea who it is recognized you?"

"No. I got a note saying they knew I was Frank James."

"What did the person ask for?"

"That's just it," Frank said. "They haven't asked for a thing."

"Yet," Clint said. "How long ago did you get the note?"

"Almost six weeks ago," the other man said. "I'm surprised I haven't heard anything since then."

"On the strength of one note you sent me a telegram?"

"On the strength of one unsigned telegram you came all this way?" Frank asked.

"Okay," Clint said, "point taken."

"Maybe nothin' will happen," Frank said.

"Why would somebody recognize you, let you know and then not do anything about it?"

"I don't know."

"They're going to want money," Clint said. "Or they have a grudge and they figure on making you sweat."

Frank snapped his fingers. "That must be it. Somebody with an old grudge against me and Jesse."

"It would probably be better if it was somebody who wanted money," Clint pointed out.

"Why?"

"Because somebody with a grudge will probably try to kill you. I think you better start carrying a gun, Frank."

"That's why I want you to stay," Frank said. "So you're the one carryin' it."

"I'll watch your back," Clint said, "but I'm not going to be a bodyguard."

"Why not?"

"Because the bodyguard becomes a target," Clint said. "If you wear a gun you accomplish two things."

"Name 'em."

"First, the person behind all this sees you with a gun and knows you're not going to just roll over."

"And second?"

"You have a better chance of staying alive."

Dan Chapman was walking past the Reddick office when his boss stepped outside.

"Where's Adams, Chappy?"

"He's in with Frank."

"Doin' what?"

Chapman shrugged. "Beats me. Frank shared some food with us and then told me to go to work. That's where I'm goin'."

"Okay," Reddick said. "You can go."

"Yes, sir."

Reddick turned to go back inside and stopped when he saw Gloria Augustus coming towards him.

"Gloria," he said, when she'd reached him.

"Hello, Bill," she said. "I'm looking for Clint Adams."

"He's in with my foreman," Reddick said. "Why do you want to see him?"

"I . . . I just wanted to talk to him about Earl."

"How's the boy doing?"

"He's resting," she said. "I think he'll be all right."

"Well . . . do you know where Frank Howard's shack is?"

"I think so."

"That's where you'll find Adams."

"All right," she said. "Thanks."

He watched her as she walked away. Gloria was the finest looking woman Reddick had ever met. She was also trouble.

• • •

"Come on, Frank," Clint said. "You're just inviting a bullet if you walk around unarmed."

"How do I explain suddenly wantin' to carry a gun?"

"Tell anyone who asks that you're nervous ever since Earl and I got shot at."

Frank scratched his beard.

"That could work, I guess. And you'll stay around and watch my back?"

"For a while, yes," Clint said. "I'll also nose around and see if I can find out who sent you the note. Was there anything helpful in the note, itself?"

"Just my name and Jesse's name," Frank said. "And the words 'I know who you are.' "

"Well," Clint said. "I guess that's plain enough."

Frank was about to respond when there was a knock at the door. The two men looked at each other.

"I'll answer it," Clint said. "I've got the gun. By the way, where is yours?"

"In that trunk, against the wall."

"Well, you'd better get it out and strap it on," Clint said and went to answer the door.

TWENTY-NINE

Clint was surprised to find Gloria Augustus standing in the doorway when he opened the door. Behind him Frank had retrieved his gunbelt from the wooden chest and was strapping it on. When he saw Gloria he paused, set the gunbelt down on top of the chest.

"Well, hello," Clint said. "What a coincidence."

"Not such a coincidence," she said. "I was looking for you. Somebody told me you were here."

"And who would that be?" he asked. The only person who knew he was there was Chapman.

"Bill Reddick."

That was okay. He could have heard it from Chappy.

"Hello, Frank," she said, looking past Clint.

"Mrs. Augustus."

"Are you finished with Mr. Adams?" she asked. "I'd like to talk to him."

124

"I think we're done," Clint said, looking at Frank. "Are we finished, Frank?"

"I—I think so."

"So then I'll see you around."

"You will?"

"Yes," Clint said. "I will. That gun looks like it could use some oil." Clint could see that from across the shack.

"I'll take care of it."

"You do that."

Clint stepped outside and pulled the door of the shack closed behind him.

"What does he need with a gun?" she asked. "I've never seen him carry one before."

"He heard about Earl getting shot," Clint said. "I guess he just wants to be able to protect himself."

"He's a miner," she said, "not a gunman. He'll probably shoot his foot off."

"Yes, he probably will," Clint said. They were standing in the mud in front of the shack. "What did you want to talk to me about?"

"Oh, this and that . . . Earl . . ."

"We should go someplace cleaner," he said. "You're going to get your dress dirty."

She looked down at herself. The dress was a simple one, with a high neck, tucked in at the waist. She was long and lean, with breasts like ripe peaches.

"I don't think I own a clean dress," she said. "That wasn't something I anticipated when we came here from back East."

"Somebody should have warned you."

"Yes," she said. "Somebody should have."

"Is there a place where we can get a cup of coffee?"

"There are a couple of places that serve food."

"Why don't you lead the way, then?"

"Okay, I will."

She turned, and her first step put her foot right into a hole. She lost her balance, but Clint grabbed her arms and kept her from falling over.

"Thank you," she said, somewhat breathlessly. "I just can't seem to get used to these holes."

"I'll just hold onto your arm—if that's all right."

"Oh, yes," she said, "I think that would be . . . fine."

She led him to a small tent just off the main street. As they entered he was hit by both the smell of food cooking and the heat. Both were not unpleasant.

"Before we sit," he said, "is this all right?"

"What do you mean?"

"Well . . . you're a married woman."

"So?"

"It's just that . . . I'm a strange man . . . with a bit of a reputation—" he stammered.

"A bit of one?" she asked. "I would say you have one of the bigger reputations in the West, wouldn't you?"

"I wouldn't like to say that, no," he replied, "but you're probably right."

"In any case, I'm still a single man sitting with a married woman. Maybe your husband won't—"

"My husband will understand that we're talking

about poor Earl," she assured him. "After all, you're paying for his room while he recovers."

"That's true."

"And I'll have to visit him over there to check his wound."

"Also true."

"So you and I will have to talk from time to time, while you're here. Why not do it in comfort?"

"Why not?"

There were tables spread out in the room, some of which looked handmade. About half of them were occupied, so they had their choice. There was an empty table near a potbellied stove so Clint chose it and walked Gloria over. He held her chair, then sat across from her with his back to the stove. The heat on his back was not his only aim, there was also the cover the cast iron stove offered. It was the best he could do sitting inside of a tent, where there were no wood walls to put his back to.

"Are you comfortable enough?"

"Comfortable," he said. "Not enough, but it'll do."

A tired-looking woman in her fifties came over to take their order.

"Just coffee for me, Hetty."

"Me, too," Clint said.

Hetty gave them a look and Clint thought he saw a small smile pass between her and Gloria.

"Friend of yours?" he asked.

"The decent women in town have sort of banded together," she said. "We all feel that we were duped into coming here."

"Duped?"

"By our husbands. They never warned us about the conditions here."

"Maybe it's your husbands who were duped."

"That may be," she said, "but they passed it on to us."

"And what's this about decent women?"

"The whores don't count."

"They're not women?"

"Not decent women," she said. "And they knew what they were in for when they were brought here."

"So the decent women don't consort with the whores?"

"Do they in any town?"

"Now that you mention it, no."

"Back East it was different," she said. "Some of the madams were members of high society. They'd go to dinner in fancy restaurants, go to the theater . . . they had money and standing."

"There's a lot of difference between here and the East," Clint said.

"Well, one thing isn't different," she said.

"And what would that be?"

"Men."

"What about them?"

"The special ones are rare."

"Is your husband one of the special ones?"

"Oh, Lord, no," she said. "But you are. I could see that the moment we met."

"Well," he said, "I think you're pretty special, too, Gloria."

"Good," she said, with a pretty smile, "that's good. We're thinking alike."

"Are we?" he asked.

She gave him a look he could only describe as hungry. "Oh, I think we are."

Hetty came back with the coffee, but as much steam as there was rising from the two cups, she thought there was more heat passing between Clint and Gloria.

THIRTY

"We're not here to talk about Earl, are we?" Clint asked Gloria Augustus.

"No."

"What are we here to talk about?"

"You."

For a moment Clint became confused. Could he have mistaken Gloria's interest in him?

"What about me?"

"You're an unusual man," she said. "I told you, I'm not used to meeting unusual men."

"Was your husband unusual when you met him?"

She seemed taken aback by the question. She sat back in her chair and stared at him for a moment.

"Jerrod?" She thought a moment. "I suppose he was. He was rich and powerful."

"That's not unusual back East where you came from, is it?" Clint asked. "What's that accent I hear? Philadelphia?"

She blinked at him in surprise.

"That's very good. You've been to Philadelphia?"

"Once or twice," he admitted.

"And where else?"

"All over." He shrugged. "Boston, New York, Baltimore."

"More and more surprising," she said. "I thought you men of the West tended to stay in the West?"

He didn't bother telling her that, a long time ago, he too had come West from the East. She really didn't need to know that, and there was nothing left back there for him, anyway.

"Well, this man of the West does tend to travel a bit."

She was looking at him with new eyes.

"What is it you want from me, Gloria?" he asked. "It's not a ticket out of here you're looking for, is it?"

"Oh, my, yes," she said. "From almost the first moment we arrived—but I'm not looking at you as a ticket out, so don't worry about that."

"Then what is it you want?"

She sat forward, leaned on the table.

"Shall I be very frank?" she asked. "Bold, even?"

"Please do."

She looked around to make sure no one was within earshot.

"Sex."

"What?"

"Sex," she said, again. "That's what I want from you."

"You have a husband."

"So?"

"And . . ."

"And what?"

"Well . . . I've heard stories."

"Already?" she asked. "About me?"

"Yes."

"Well, they're probably true," she said.

"About you and . . . what's his name? Your husband's foreman? Kyle?"

"Derrick has been . . . useful to me in the past," she said.

"It doesn't sound like you've been very discreet."

"On the contrary," she said. "We've been very discreet."

"But . . . your husband knows?"

"My husband knows as little or as much as he wants to know," she told him.

"And how is that?"

"He asks," she said, "and when he asks, I tell him. It's part of the arrangement we have."

"That's . . . quite an arrangement."

"Well, he couldn't very well expect me to stay in this hellhole without some entertainment."

"So, when you have sex with Derrick Kyle, you tell your husband all about it?"

"Yes."

"And does Kyle know about the arrangement?"

"Oh, Lord, no," she said. "I could never tell him about it."

"Why?"

"Because he's in love with me," she said. "He thinks he's going to take me away from all this."

"And he's not?"

"No," she said. "He's not man enough."

"Gloria—"

"Now, you'd be man enough to take me away from here—"

"I'm not—"

"But that's not what I want from you."

He fell silent.

"All I want is sex."

"But you can get that from Derrick Kyle," he said. "And, I suspect, some other men up here."

"Miners," she said, making a face. "Men with rough hands and dirt beneath their fingernails."

"So you sleep with Kyle because he has clean hands?"

"He was the compromise my husband and I came up with."

"So then, let me ask you this."

She waited.

"If we went to bed together, would you be telling your husband about it?"

"Oh, no," she said. "This would be our little secret."

"And in a mining town this small, would you be able to keep a secret like this?"

"I would."

"You're sure?"

"Very sure."

Hetty came over and poured them some more coffee. The older woman gave Gloria another look before going away.

"Somehow," Clint said, "I don't think that's true."

"Oh," she said, "it wouldn't be a secret from someone like Hetty."

"And some of the other wives?"

Gloria smiled.

"We swap stories," she said. "For instance, Hetty stays after closing and has sex with Mike Dudley. He owns this place, does all the cooking and takes care of her needs."

"And her husband?"

"He works in my husband's mine."

"And what about Mr. Dudley," he asked. "Does he have a wife?"

"No."

"But he could visit the whores."

"He could indeed," she agreed, "but he's cheap and doesn't want to pay them. So he and Hetty have come to an arrangement."

"And the other wives?" he asked. "Some of them have the same kind of arrangements?"

"Yes."

"And you all talk about it."

"We have to," she said. "We'd go insane, otherwise."

"So if you and I were to . . ."

"Oh, I'd have to tell them," she said. "How could I have sex with the infamous Gunsmith and not tell my friends?"

THIRTY-ONE

While Gloria Augustus was trying to convince Clint Adams to have sex with her, Arvard Turner was trying to get into Red Mountain Town without being seen. Unfortunately, that meant getting down in the mud, staying low so that no one saw him until he was ready for them to.

Arvard was looking for two men he knew he could buy. The last two had been terrible shots with a gun and had been more trouble than they were worth. One had gotten himself killed, and Arvard himself had to put the other one in the ground. This time he needed to find two men he knew could handle a gun and who would understand that killing Clint Adams had to be done for more than just money. Killing the Gunsmith was a rep maker. Anyone who couldn't understand that was a fool.

Most of the men in Red Mountain Town were just

miners, but luckily not all of them. All he needed to do was find two men who weren't.

"Mrs. Augustus—"

"I thought you were going to call me Gloria?" she objected.

"Gloria, I don't usually make it a habit to sleep with married women, not even beautiful ones."

"You think I'm beautiful?"

"Don't be coy—"

"No, no, it's not that," she assured him. "It's just that—" She stopped and touched her face. "I know I was beautiful in Philadelphia, and when I left Philadelphia, even when we arrived here. But now, after months of exposure up here, my skin . . . it's so dry. I must look like old leather."

"I think you know that's not true, Gloria," Clint said.

"Well . . . it feels like leather." She leaned forward. "Feel my cheek."

"That wouldn't be very discreet, would it?" he asked.

She sat back in her chair and glared at him.

"Are you going to sit there and tell me you don't want to sleep with me?" she demanded.

"No, I can't tell you that," he replied, honestly. "From the first moment I saw you I wondered what it would be like to sleep with you."

"Well, there . . ." she said, with a wide smile. "That wasn't so very hard to admit, was it?"

"No, it wasn't."

"Now all that remains is the when and the where?" she said.

That wasn't exactly all that remained. He was thinking that as nice as it would be to have sex with Gloria Augustus it might be even nicer to find out everything she knew about what was going on in Red Mountain Town. There was a truth about men and sex that was inescapable: they talked in bed. So it was probably the women in town—the underappreciated wives—who knew everything that was going on. Maybe one of them knew who had recognized Frank Howard as Frank James.

Of course, this was a poor reason to have sex with a married woman but it sure didn't sound as if her husband was that concerned—and she was a beautiful woman.

"All right," he said. "Let's go."

"Now?"

"Now's as good a time as any," he said. "I told you, I've been imagining you naked since I first saw you."

He was surprised to see her blush crimson.

"No, you didn't tell me that, exactly," she said, squirming in her chair, "but I like the sound of it."

"So if the time is now," he said, "where's the place?"

"Just give me a minute."

She got up, walked across the room—or the "tent"—and put her head together with Hetty who, Clint noticed now for the first time, was a rather handsome woman, although an older and completely different type from Gloria.

She came back to the table and sat down.

"I'm going to leave," she said. "You stay here and wait for Hetty to come for you."

"Hetty?"

"She'll take you out the back," Gloria said. "Follow her directions."

"Okay."

"Shake my hand before I leave," she said. "It'll look more businesslike."

Clint stood up and took Gloria's hand. Her flesh was hot and she shivered as they touched.

"Oh, my," she said, and then left, breathing rapidly.

Clint sat back down and finished his coffee.

Frank James sat in his shack, working his gun over with a rag and some gun oil. The gun in his hand was his brother's old .44 Schofield. His mother had taken to selling Jesse's guns for money—and selling some guns that weren't really Jesse's—but Frank had saved this one for himself. Handling it made him feel like part of his brother was still there with him.

He hadn't fired the gun in a very long time, but Clint was right. He had to be prepared to protect himself. Still, he felt good having Clint there to watch his back. Nobody had ever watched it for him the way Jesse had, but Clint would come a close second.

Clint Adams was now the only living man he trusted, and he was trusting him with his life.

Before long Hetty came over to Clint's table and smiled at him. She looked tired, but her skin was pale and smooth. Working inside kept her from the elements, but he was sure that, like Gloria, she probably thought her looks were suffering.

"I'm Hetty."

"I know," he said. "Clint."

"I know. Are you ready?" she asked. She seemed extremely amused by the whole thing.

"I'm ready."

"Pay me, then get up and follow me."

He paid her for the coffee and followed her to the kitchen portion of the tent where the heat was more intense. There was a potbellied man—a rock-hard belly, not something soft and squishy—standing at a stove. He was unshaven and, when he grinned at Clint and gave him a lascivious wink, there were spaces where teeth were missing. Clint simply nodded back to the man.

Hetty took him out a black flap so that they were standing outside the tent. The cool air was now welcome after the heat of the kitchen.

"Walk along here, stay behind the buildings. Before long you'll come to a clearing with a small shack. If there's smoke coming from the chimney, go on in."

"Smoke."

"That's the all clear."

"And is this a shack you, uh, all use?"

"A lot of us," she said. "Don't judge us, mister. We're doin' what we gotta do to survive in this place."

"Believe me, Hetty," he said. "I'm the last person you have to worry about judging you."

"And you be good to Gloria," she said. "She's a good woman. You do anythin' to hurt her, you're gonna have to answer to me and a bunch of other women here in Red Mountain. We're real protective of each other around here."

"I'll keep that in mind."

She hesitated, then looked around before reaching her hand behind his neck and pulling him down to her for a kiss—a real kiss, with soft lips and a lively tongue. Right in the midst of the surprisingly pleasant and enjoyable kiss he thought that the cook was a lucky guy.

When she released him she was breathless and flushed.

"Sorry," she said. "Just takin' a taste for myself. Gloria said it would be okay."

"You won't hear me complaining, Hetty," he said.

"You go along now," she said, "before I change my mind and keep you for myself."

THIRTY-TWO

When Clint reached the clearing he saw a small shack that resembled the one Frank James was living in as Frank Howard. There was a stove pipe stuck in the ceiling as a chimney, and white smoke was billowing from it. He paused for a moment, considering. He could be walking into a trap where he'd find men with guns instead of a naked Gloria Augustus. However, the prospect of not only seeing Gloria naked but being with her almost made it worth the risk. Besides, he recalled the way she had blushed earlier, and he didn't think a woman—or a man— could fake something like that.

He crossed the clearing and approached the front door of the shack. Sleeping with married women was not a habit with his, but he consoled himself with the fact that he might be getting some information that would help Frank. If he had to have sex with a gorgeous woman to get it, so be it. No sacrifice was too great for a friend.

He opened the front door of the shack and entered. The warmth from inside was not as intense as it had been in the kitchen Hetty had walked him through, but it was pleasant. So was the sight of a nude Gloria waiting for him on the bed.

"Right on time," she said.

"Am I?"

"I was getting anxious," she admitted. "I thought you might change your mind."

She shivered, reminding him to close the door behind him. Or maybe she was shivering for another reason.

As he approached the bed she got to her knees and he was able to get a good look at her. Her breasts were small, but solid and round, with pink nipples. Her skin was smooth and pale, her hips slender. He knew if she'd been standing he'd see long, slender legs. She looked like some dancers he'd once seen on stage, long, lithe and graceful.

"You're beautiful," he said.

"Come to me," she said. "Take off all those clothes. I feel like I've been waiting forever for you."

He reached for his gunbelt, then hesitated. Putting himself in this position was not without risk. He had to depend on Gloria's word that this was a secret place she and her friends used, but a secret became less of one when more than one person knew it.

"Don't worry," she said. "It's safe." She got off the

bed, walked up to him and began to undo the buckle. "You're safe here from everyone . . . except me."

"Who says I want to be safe from you?" he asked. He leaned over to taste her lips, then her neck and shoulders. Her flesh became dappled with goose bumps, and this time he knew it had nothing to do with the cold.

Sam Burnett and Al Maxx entered the largest tent in Red Mountain Town, the one that housed the place everybody called the Saloon. They went to the bar, got themselves a beer and then took a table. Before long somebody appeared at their table, and it wasn't a saloon girl.

"Jesus Christ," Burnett said, "you look like you've been rolling around in the mud, Arvard. What the hell are you doin'?"

"Don't say my name so loud," Arvard said, pulling up a chair.

"You ain't gonna drink with us lookin' like that," Maxx said.

"I don't wanna drink, I just gotta talk to you fellas."

"About what."

"Clint Adams." Burnett and Maxx exchanged a look.

"What about the Gunsmith?" Maxx asked.

"He's in town."

"Is that right?" Burnett asked.

"And I need help to kill him."

"And what's in it for us?" Burnett asked.

"Bein' the men who killed Clint Adams."

"You don't want the credit?" Maxx asked.

"No."

"Why not?"

"You gettin' paid a lot for this, Arvard?" Burnett asked.

"No, I ain't," Arvard said. "I just gotta kill him."

"And you don't care if we take the credit," Maxx repeated.

"That's right."

Again, the two partners exchanged a look. They both knew Arvard Turner was a little weasel who didn't do nothing for nothing.

"Somethin' ain't right here, Sam," Maxx said.

"Now, now, Al," Burnett said, "let's give Arvard the benefit of the doubt. He needs to have Adams dead for some reason."

"Let's put it this way," Arvard said. "If Adams ain't dead soon, I will be."

"There," Burnett said to Maxx. "Now that sounds like a good reason, don't it?"

"The best."

Burnett turned his attention back to Arvard.

"When do you want this done?"

"As soon as possible."

"Are we gonna do it, or are we gonna back your play?"

"I don't care," Arvard said. "The three of us can do it, you two can do it, or you two can decide which one of you is gonna do it. I don't care, as long as he ends up dead."

"Why don't you do it yourself?"

"I can't do it alone."

"I thought you were good with a gun," Maxx said.

"I am."

"But not as good as the Gunsmith?" Burnett asked.

"I don't know."

"And you don't want to find out," Burnett said.

Arvard didn't speak.

Burnett looked at Maxx.

Maxx looked at Burnett.

"You want to find out, Al?" Burnett asked.

"Hell, no," Burnett said. "I ain't about to face him alone. But I'll back your play, Sam."

"That's tempting," Burnett said. "Very tempting."

"So? How about it?" Arvard asked.

"We'll let you know later."

"Later? When later?"

"In the morning."

"What am I supposed to do until then?" Arvard complained.

"Get cleaned up," Burnett said. "Don't come near us lookin' like that again."

"Yeah," Maxx said. "You'll ruin our reputations."

Arvard regarded the two men who were unshaven and filthy themselves from riding the trail—filthy, but not quite as muddy as he was.

"Go on, Arvard," Burnett said, "we're tryin' to attract a little female attention, here."

"Okay, okay," Arvard said, "but I'll look for you fellas here tomorrow."

"Sure," Burnett said, "tomorrow."

They both watched as Arvard slunk out of the saloon, thinking no one saw him.

"Whataya think?" Maxx asked.

"It's interesting."

"What about him?"

"He's gettin' somethin' out of this," Burnett said. "And whatever it is, we'll get it out of him, after the job is done."

"You think you can do it, Sam?"

"Do what?"

"Face the Gunsmith," Maxx said. "Beat him, I mean. You think you can outdraw him?"

"Like I said," Burnett repeated, "it's a real interestin' thought."

"So we're gonna do it?"

"Sure, why not?" Burnett said. "All we gotta do is figure how—but right now, I want a bath and a woman."

"In that order?"

"Maybe together," Burnett said. "At the same time."

"I don't want no bath," Maxx said, "but I'll take a woman."

Both Arvard and the Gunsmith were forgotten for the time being.

THIRTY-THREE

Clint was naked and in the bed with Gloria, his gun-belt hanging within easy reach on the bedpost. Their legs were entwined and their hands were roaming everywhere as they became acquainted with each other's bodies.

"There's no reason to rush this," she'd told him.

"What about your husband?" he asked. "It's getting late. Won't he be expect—"

She pressed her finger to his lips to quiet him.

"I told you, my husband is not a problem."

"But if you don't come home, he'll think you're with Derrick Kyle, right?"

"Possibly."

"And what happens if he asks Kyle—"

"He won't."

Clint finally decided just to take her word for it: they had a lot of time for this, and there was no reason to rush.

And once his hands and mouth experienced her skin, he didn't want to rush. She was like scented silk, and when he slid his hand down over her belly to cup her hairy mound, she tensed and moaned. He rubbed his palm over her until she became wet, and then he touched her with his fingers.

"Oh . . . my . . . God," she said. "Your fingers are like magic. You've done this to women before."

"Once or twice," he admitted.

He continued to stroke her until his own impatience overcame him. He kissed her breasts, her nipples, then worked his way down her body until he removed his fingers and replaced them with his lips and tongue. He licked and nibbled at her until she had soaked the sheet between them, and then abruptly she pushed his head away forcefully and said, "Oooh, wait, wait, stop . . ."

She pushed herself away from him and huddled near the top of the bed in an almost fetal position.

"What's wrong?"

Her whole body was flushed, her lips swollen and her nostrils flaring as she hugged herself.

"Too good, damnit," she swore, "that was too good. You're trying to kill me."

"Gloria—"

"Give me a minute," she said, and then laughed. "I'm serious, you know. I've never felt anything like that. It was too . . . damn . . . good."

He sat back and gave her some space.

"I have to admit," he said. "I've never heard that before. I never knew sex could be too good."

"Well, when you've been with the men I've been with," she began, "men who are too concerned about their own pleasure to give a damn about mine . . ."

"Men should know that the better they make a woman feel the better she'll make them feel."

She stared at him as if he'd just spoken a foreign language.

"I've been with a lot of men, Clint Adams," she said. "I've never known one who thinks the way you do."

She unfurled herself and crawled across the bed to him. She got to her knees, put her hands on his shoulders and used all her strength and weight to push him down on his back.

"My turn," she said.

"Yes, ma'am."

He got comfortable on his back while she began to make love to his body with her hands, her mouth and her tongue. She licked the length of his rigid penis, getting it good and wet before sliding it between her lips and taking the entire length into her mouth. She moaned as she sucked him, her head bobbing, her mouth riding up and down on him.

Clint stared down at her head and relished the feeling of her lips riding him up and down. She slid her hands beneath his butt at one point, apparently trying to get him even deeper into her mouth. He lifted his ass off the bed to try to help her. She continued to suckle him until he was ready to burst, then abruptly released him.

She scrambled up on top of him, as if she were

afraid he'd go soft if she didn't hop on quickly. Grabbing his penis, she pressed the spongy head against her moist portal and then eased herself down on him. He entered her easily and her insides were like a furnace. She gasped as he pierced her to the core, her eyes going wide. She pressed her palms down on his belly and started riding him . . .

Jerrod Augustus was annoyed for two reasons. One, he didn't know where his wife was. Two, he cared.

They shared a small house in town—possibly the cleanest house in town, inside and out, because he had people keep it clean for her. He tried to do things to keep her happy, but he seemed to fail miserably every time. When he agreed to allow her to sleep with his foreman, he was making the supreme sacrifice to make her happy, but even that didn't seem to work. Maybe Derrick Kyle wasn't man enough for her in bed. God knew he wasn't, but that was because he was so much older than she was. She had married him for his money. He knew that and didn't care. Their deal was she could spend his money as long as she did what a wife was supposed to do—and that included coming to Colorado with him.

However, since arriving in Colorado she had been extremely unhappy and nothing he said or did made a difference. Lately, however, he'd started to care a bit more than he used to. Now he wondered where she was and what she was doing, because he knew for a fact that Derrick Kyle was in the mine.

He decided to go to the rooming house to check on Earl. Maybe Gloria was with him.

• • •

Gloria was on her back with her legs spread, her ankles were in Clint Adams's hands. He had her spread as wide as she could be and was thrusting himself in and out of her, grunting with the effort.

"That's it," she urged him, "that's it, hard, harder . . . don't be afraid . . . I won't . . . break . . ."

The smell in the air as well as the sight of her— she appeared to be more naked, for some reason, than any other woman he'd ever been with—along with her urgings were driving him on. He felt harder than he'd ever felt, and thought that he might not ever explode. His erection was almost painful as he continued to drive into her.

"Yeah, that's it," she said, "that's what I want . . . Oh my God, finally a man who can satisfy me . . ."

"I'll satisfy you," he said. He just hoped he didn't satisfy himself into an early grave doing it!

THIRTY-FOUR

"It's dark out," Clint said.

He'd finally managed to wear Gloria out. For a woman who had pushed him away in the beginning because the sex felt "too good," she had recovered easily and managed to last very nicely through some "damn good" sex.

"I should go," she said. "Do you have a place to stay?"

"I took a room in the same place we put Earl," he reminded her.

"You can stay here if you like and save the money."

"No," he said. "I'll stay over there. Besides, what if one of your friends wants to use this place? I don't want to be the one who messes with the status quo."

"Well, I'll leave first, then," she said and got up from the bed.

He watched with pleasure as she pulled her dress

back on. He enjoyed watching women dress. She moved smoothly, gracefully, and he saw that he'd been right about her legs. They were almost impossibly long.

While she dressed he tried to nonchalantly ask some questions.

"Gloria," he said, "you seem to know what's going on up here."

"I should," she said. "I don't have anything to do all day but listen to everyone talk."

"So what is going on?" he asked.

She paused in a bent over position, her breasts swaying. He almost forgot the question.

"What do you mean?"

"Well . . . somebody taking shots at me and Earl, putting a bullet in the poor kid's shoulder. There's got to be a reason."

"What about your reputation?" she asked, moving again. She turned her back to him to don her dress, but that didn't help at all. She had a beautiful back and a gorgeous ass. He watched them both disappear into the dress.

"That's possible," he said, "but what if somebody thought I was coming here because I was hired to?"

She laughed and turned to face him.

"Somehow I don't see you as a miner."

"Well, not as a miner, then?"

"Then as wha—oh, I see. You think somebody might think you'd been hired for your gun. Well, who would do that? I mean, hire you for your gun?"

"I don't know," he said. "That's why I was asking you."

"I don't know," she said. "I suppose somebody could think that Reddick would hire you."

"To do what?"

"To kill my husband?" The question seemed to excite her. "You're not here to kill Jerrod, are you?"

"No."

"Did Jerrod hire you to kill Reddick?"

"No."

She shrugged. "Then I don't know."

"Do you think one of the other wives might have heard something?" he asked, carefully.

She walked to the bed to kiss him good night and said, "I suppose they might, but you'd have to ask them."

"Maybe I will."

She laughed and touched his face, then put her hand on his chest.

"You might have to give them a little of what you gave me tonight to get them to talk to you. Already Hetty is interested."

"Hetty? I thought she had her boyfriend the cook."

"Did you see him when you left that tent?"

"Well, yeah—"

"Believe me," she said. "She wants you."

"Well, I don't think—"

"I'll check on Earl first thing in the morning," she promised, cutting him off. "Will I see you?"

"I'll be there."

"And don't worry," she said. "Hetty won't tell a soul about us, and neither will I."

"Except the other wives, right?"

"Um, well, yes," she said, "except for them, but they won't tell anyone, either."

As she left the shack Clint wondered if he'd just made a mistake—a huge, pleasurable mistake.

He was sitting on the bed, reaching for his trousers when the door to the shack abruptly opened. He thought it was Gloria coming back, but he reached for his gun, anyway.

"Did you forget something—" He stopped when he saw that his visitor wasn't Gloria.

"Oh, hello, Hetty."

"Hello, Mr. Adams." She had an odd look on her face. It took him a moment to place it, but then it became clear. She was aroused. She probably wanted to use the shack with her friend, the cook.

"I'll be out of here in a minute," he said, then realized he was naked. He'd have to stand up to pull his trousers on.

"Don't leave on my account," she said.

"Well, I don't want to be in the way if you and the cook want to—"

"Cook's not coming," she said, reaching for the buttons on her dress.

"What? Hetty—"

"It's just you and me now, mister," she said, peeling the dress down to her waist.

He was going to protest, but stopped when he saw her breasts. They were large and full, her smooth skin darker than Gloria's and her nipples the brown of pennies.

"I've been waitin' outside for Gloria to finish with you."

After Gloria he'd thought he was finished for the night but the sight of this woman's body as she peeled the dress off the rest of the way . . . she was thick-waisted, with a dark tangle of hair between her heavy thighs, and from across the room he could smell the tang of her readiness.

"I'm a lusty woman, Mr. Adams," she said. "I ain't young, but I ain't dried up. I'll bet you can tell that from there. Can you smell me?"

"Hetty . . . yes, I can."

She laughed, a deep-throated, bawdy laugh and he felt chills run down his spine. Maybe it was the woman, or the situation, or both, but suddenly he had a rock hard erection springing up from his lap, which Hetty could plainly see.

"I'm thinkin' that there's for me, Mr. Adams," she told him, "and I aim to have it."

THIRTY-FIVE

"Where have you been?" Jerrod Augustus asked as Gloria entered their small house.

"I've been with Earl," she said. "The poor boy was running a fever. He really should see a doctor."

"Maybe Adams can take him down to Ouray tomorrow," Augustus said. He knew she was lying. He had gone to see Earl. And Mrs. Philby, the woman who ran the rooming house, said she hadn't seen Gloria since she and "that man" had brought Earl in. She sniffed when she said Gloria's name, as if she were smelling something bad.

Augustus then went home to wait for his wife. Now he wasn't sure whether he should call her on her lie or not. He wasn't sure he wanted to hear the truth.

"I have a question for you, Jerrod."

"What's that, my dear?"

"Did you hire this man, Clint Adams, to come here for some reason?"

"What reason would I have to hire a gunman?"

"I don't know," she said. "To get rid of Bill Reddick?"

"Reddick and I are competitors, it's true," Augustus said, "but that doesn't mean I want to kill him."

"Well, what about him?"

"Reddick?"

"Would he hire a gunman to kill you?"

Augustus started to speak, then hesitated.

"You think Bill Reddick brought the Gunsmith here to kill me?" he asked, slowly.

"I don't know, Jerrod," she said. "I was asking you. I'm going to go and take a bath."

As she left the room Augustus was suddenly less interested in where his wife had been and more interested in where the Gunsmith was.

Hetty approached Clint, got to her knees in front of him and put her hands on his thighs. Her eyes were on the column of flesh that jutted up at her from between his legs.

Slowly she took him in one hand, sliding her fingers up and down the length of him, all the while looking him in the eyes.

"Hetty—" he said, but his resolve was all but gone.

"I wasn't always a waitress, you know," she said. "When I was younger, I was like some of these other girls in camp. I was a whore and a good one. But even though that was many years ago, I haven't forgotten how to satisfy a man. Only, for all the time I've been in this godforsaken camp, I haven't found a man I wanted to satisfy."

"Your husband—"

"Isn't interested in sex anymore," she said. "He's only interested in gold."

"And the cook—"

"That's Hal," she said, rubbing her right palm on his thigh while pumping him lightly with her left. "He's sweet, but he doesn't know what to do with a woman. According to Gloria, you do."

"You talked with Gloria?"

She smiled.

"As soon as she left," she answered. "She told me about you, and from what I can see, so far, she was right." She looked at his penis then, leaned over and kissed it, then flicked it just beneath the head with the tip of her tongue. It felt like he'd been struck by lightning. Then, she swooped down and engulfed him with her mouth. She continued to encircle the base of his cock with her right hand, while with her left she fondled his testicles. Gloria had been very good, but this woman really knew what she was doing.

She moaned, bringing her head up and down, and when she had him good and wet, she let him slip from her lips and took him between her full breasts.

"Oh, Jesus," he said, as she roiled him between her tits, basically letting him fuck her breasts.

"Lie back," she told him, pushing him down on the bed. "Mamma's gonna make you squirm."

And she did . . .

•   •   •

Sam Burnett and Al Maxx looked at the man seated across from them.

"Frank James," Burnett said. "Are you sure?"

"I'm positive," he said. "I was in Tulsa one year and saw both him and his brother."

Al Maxx whistled soundlessly. First Clint Adams and now Frank James. The little town of Ouray, Colorado, was suddenly filling up with legends of the West.

"What do you want us to do?" Burnett asked.

"Nothin', right now," the man said, "but somethin's gonna happen in the next few days. I'll need you boys to back my play."

"And what's in it for us?" Maxx asked.

"Aside from being the men who killed Frank James?" the man asked.

"We're not lookin' to become two more Bob Fords, ya know," Burnett said. "Killin' Jesse James hasn't turned out so good for him."

"Money," the man said. "There's money in it for you. A lot of it."

"Now you're talkin'," Maxx said.

"What about Clint Adams?" Burnett asked.

The man sat back in his chair.

"How did you know he was in town?"

"Word gets around," Maxx said. "Can't hide a man with a reputation like that."

"Is he involved in this Frank James thing?"

"No."

"Are you sure?" Maxx asked.

"Adams is here by coincidence."

"You're sure of that?" Burnett asked.

The man hesitated, then said, "No, I can't be sure, but he's not here because of my business."

"So you don't have any objection if we go after Adams while we're here?" Maxx asked.

"I don't object," the man said, "as long as you handle my business first."

"And when will that be?" Burnett asked.

"Soon," the man said. "Don't worry. I'll let you know."

THIRTY-SIX

As it turned out, Clint did end up spending the night in that shack. He was just too worn out after Hetty left to even get dressed.

Hetty had thoroughly enjoyed Clint's hard dick, suckling it and cooing to it, stroking it until he couldn't take it anymore. He reversed their position, put her on her back and started doing the same to her. Her breasts were remarkably firm for a woman her age, the nipples thick and chewy. He spent a lot of time on those two impressive mounds before moving down to the black jungle of hair between her thighs. She was thoroughly wet by then and he drove his tongue deep into that snatch, licking and sucking until she tensed and cried out and held his head in place while waves of pleasure flowed over her and through her.

"Jesus," she gasped, still holding his head tightly, "don't stop . . . God, don't stop . . ."

He continued to suck on her, lick up all her juices, until finally her body relaxed and she released his head. He wasn't done, though. He got between her thick thighs, spread her legs apart and drove himself into her. He pounded away at her as she wrapped her powerful legs around him, and then she pulled his head down to her so she could kiss him while he fucked her. Her kisses were amazing, long, deep, wet kisses that went on even when they were both spent, after he had exploded inside of her. She obviously loved kissing and was very good at it.

He fell asleep and woke when she leaned down to kiss him again. She had already gotten dressed.

"I'll tell Gloria she was right," she promised him.

"Wait," he said, "before you go . . ."

She sat down on the bed next to him, placed her hand on his belly.

"What is it?"

"I'm concerned about the shooting," he said. "I don't know if you heard—"

"About poor Earl bein' shot?" she asked. "I hear pretty much everythin' there is to hear in this town, darlin'."

"That's my point, Hetty," he said. "I'm wondering what you have heard about it."

"Well, nothin' up till now," she said, "but I'll keep my ears open for you." Her hand began to move lower.

"That'd be great," he said, as her hand encircled his semihard dick. "I'd, uh, appreciate it."

She continued to fondle him and stroke him until he was fully hard again.

"My God, but you're an amazin' man," she said. "Me and Gloria in one night and look at you."

He did look at himself. He was as hard as he had ever been in her hand.

"Mmm," she said, leaning over to take him in her mouth once again. She didn't rush and sucked him until he exploded into her mouth with a deep-throated cry.

"You sleep now, you beautiful man," she told him afterward. He didn't have to be told twice . . .

When he woke he looked around, for a moment not recalling where he was. Then it all came back to him and he lay there and replayed much of it. The sheets and pillows smelled of both women, and before long he was hard again.

"Jesus," he said to himself, shaking his head.

He tried to ignore his erection and got dressed. He strapped on his gun and left the shack. It appeared to be only about a half hour past dawn. He wondered if he should go to the rooming house and freshen himself, or if he'd find someplace open this early for breakfast?

Walking down the muddy main street of Red Mountain Town, he suddenly became aware of the smell in the air—eggs, if he wasn't mistaken. And potatoes. He followed the smell and was surprised that it did not lead him to the place where Hetty worked. Instead he found himself in front of a much smaller tent. For a moment he thought perhaps some-one lived there and was preparing breakfast for them-selves, but when he peered inside the flap he saw a few tables with chairs around them. He assumed the place was open to the public and stepped inside.

"Hello?" he called.

A man stuck his head out of what Clint assumed was the kitchen and grinned at him.

"Boy, you're early."

"It smelled so good it drew me here," Clint said. "That coffee I smell, too?"

"Have a seat," the man said. "I'll bring somethin' out to ya."

Clint sat at a small table with crooked legs. He considered changing, but they all looked as if they had something wrong with them. If the food tasted as good as it smelled, though, it wouldn't matter.

When the man came out he was carrying a mug and a pot of coffee. He was in his early thirties and didn't look like the type who would be running this kind of business. For one thing, he was wearing an apron—and a gun.

"Get started on this and I'll bring you a plate right away," the man said.

He poured a cup and left the pot to go back into the kitchen. The coffee was steaming hot, deep back, and just the smell of it was like ambrosia to Clint. When he tasted it, he couldn't believe it. It was possi-bly the best coffee he'd ever had.

He was pouring a second cup when the man re-turned, as promised. He had a plate heaped high with eggs and potatoes, and thick slices of ham. In his other hand he carried a plate of fresh biscuits.

"Here ya go," he said, setting the feast down in front of Clint. "You're my first customer of the day."

"I'm surprised they're not lined up outside just for this coffee," Clint said.

"Hey, thanks," the man said, wiping his hands on his apron. "So do I." As he lifted the apron, Clint got a better look at the gun. It was a clean, well-cared-for weapon. "If you like the coffee lemme know what you think of the chow."

"I sure will."

"By the way," the man said, "my name is Willie."

"Willie," Clint said, "my name's Clint Adams."

As they clasped hands Willie said, "No, really?"

"Yes, really."

"I heard you was in town," Willie said. "Jeez, the Gunsmith eatin' in my place."

Clint released the younger man's hand so he could sample the food. Around a mouthful of all three—the eggs, spuds and ham—Clint said, "I may be eating here every day while I'm here. This is great food."

"Thanks," Willie said, "thanks a lot. You just lemme know if you want more of anything. First customer of the day always pays half price."

"That a policy?"

"Sure is."

"I'm glad I happened by."

"So am I," Willie said. "I ain't never met nobody as famous as you, Mr. Adams."

"Willie," Clint said, through another mouthful, "anybody who can cook like this can call me Clint."

"Yes, sir . . . Clint."

Clint didn't want to talk anymore. He just wanted to eat.

THIRTY-SEVEN

Willie's last name was Dolan, and he was trying to launch this business all by himself, which was why it was so small. He sat down and had coffee with Clint, who remained his only customers as an hour ticked by.

"I've only been here a few weeks," he said, "but I think I can make it here. Once I'm established I'll make the place bigger."

"Why not get a partner and do it now?" Clint asked. "Seems to me with food this good you'd have it made in no time."

Willie made a face.

"I'd have to watch a partner real close, see if he was stealin' from me. I don't have time for that."

"Too bad," Clint said. "All you'd need is somebody you can trust."

"And somebody who has money."

"Hopefully," Clint added, standing up, "the same somebody. Look, let me pay you full price for this."

"No, no," Willie said, also standing. "I got to stick to my policy."

He told Clint how much the meal was and Clint paid him. It was a bargain at the price.

"Do you do supper?" Clint asked.

"I sure do."

"I'll be back."

As Clint headed for the tent flap to leave Willie called out, "Mr. Adams? Clint?"

Clint turned.

"Can I ask you to think about somethin' today?"

"Sure, what?"

Willie approached him and spoke both quickly and eagerly.

"What if I was to ask you to be my partner?"

"Willie, I don't know anything about running a restaurant."

"I'd run it," Willie said. "You'd be my silent partner. You know, the one with the money?"

"How do you know I've got money?"

"You've got to have more than I do," Willie said. "Everybody does—and it wouldn't take much for me to expand."

"Willie, I don't know. I may never be back this way once I leave," Clint explained.

"I'd send you your profits," Willie said. "Honest I would. I'm real honest."

"I'm sure you are—"

"All I'm askin' ya to do is think it over," Willie said. "You can gimme your answer later."

Clint thought a moment, then said, "Okay, I'll think it over—"

"Thank you."

"But let me ask you a question."

"What?"

"That gun," Clint said. "Why do you wear it?"

Willie looked down at his gun.

"A fella has to protect himself," he said, finally, "especially when you're in business alone."

"I notice it's real well taken care of," Clint said. "Can you use it?"

"I can usually hit what I shoot at."

"Ever shot at a man?"

"Yes."

Clint had a feeling Willie might even be more familiar with the gun than he was with pots and pans, but he decided not to push the young man any further.

"Okay."

"Okay, you'll be my partner?" Willie asked.

"Okay, I'll think it over and get back to you later," Clint said. "It's not something I want to jump right into—especially with someone I just met."

"I can tell you a lot more about myself, if you want," Willie promised him.

"I may take you up on that, Willie," Clint said. "I may just take you up on that later on."

THIRTY-EIGHT

When Clint arrived at the rooming house and knocked on the door, Mrs. Philby opened it and gave him a look of open distaste.

"I ain't givin' you your money back for last night," she said in a scolding tone. "It ain't my fault you spent the night elsewhere."

"No, it isn't, Mrs. Philby," Clint said. "I wouldn't think of asking for my money back."

"Well . . . good . . ." she said. His tone obviously puzzled her. She must have been expecting an argument.

"How's Earl?" he asked.

"How would I know?" she said. "I ain't a nurse. I ain't looked in on him."

"Well, then, I'll do that," he said. "May I come in?"

"You paid for a room here," she said, backing out of the doorway to let him enter, "but you missed breakfast."

"That's okay," Clint said. "I had breakfast elsewhere, too."

That earned him a "Hmph," after which she turned and stalked off into the kitchen.

Clint's room was on the second floor, but Earl was occupying the only first-floor room. It was 8 A.M. when Clint turned the knob and entered the room quietly. As soon as he entered he realized he needn't have tried to be quiet. Earl was awake.

"Hey," Clint said.

"'Mornin', Clint."

"How do you feel?"

"Like I been shot," Earl said. "When can I get out of here?"

"You feel up to riding?"

"No."

"Walking?"

"No."

"Then why are you worried about getting up?" Clint asked. "Besides, you've got quite a beautiful nurse looking after you?"

"Mrs. Philby?"

"No, not the landlady," Clint said. "I mean Gloria Augustus."

"I'd just as soon have Mrs. Philby," Earl said.

"Why? What's wrong with Glo—Mrs. Augustus?"

"She's trouble."

"Has Mrs. Philby been in to see you?" Clint asked.

"She brought me a cup of tea this mornin'."

So the older woman had lied to him about not checking on Earl. She was trying to hide her soft side, maybe.

"Well, Mrs. Augustus—"

"You can call her Gloria in front of me," Earl said.

"Okay," he said, "Gloria will be here soon to check on you. She'll be taking care of you until you're well enough to ride."

"Will you be around?" Earl asked.

"Yeah, I'll be staying around."

"To find out who shot me—shot at us?"

"That's right," Clint said, "to find out who shot at us. I take it real personally when somebody shoots at me, and shoots one of my friends."

Earl hesitated, then said, "We're friends?"

"That's right, Earl," Clint said. "We're friends."

"But . . . I didn't even get you here," Earl said. "That was Mr. Chapman."

"Don't worry about that, Earl," Clint said in a reassuring tone. "We're friends."

"Gee, I—"

There was a knock at the door at that moment and Gloria Augustus walked in.

"How's the patient this morning?" she asked brightly.

"Wants to know when he can get up," Clint said.

"Really?" she asked, approaching the bed. "Can you get up, Earl?"

"No, ma'am."

"Well, when you can get up . . . you can get up," she said. "Does that make sense?"

"Yes, ma'am."

"I'm going to unbandage your shoulder so I can check the wound," she told Earl. "Would you like Mr. Adams to step out?"

"No," Earl said. "Clint and I are friends. He can stay."

"All right," Gloria said, "but I just need to send him for some hot water from Mrs. Philby."

"Oh," Earl said.

"Clint?"

"I'll be right back, Earl."

"Okay."

Clint left the room and went to the kitchen to ask Mrs. Philby for a pot of hot water. To his surprise she took a pot off the stove and immediately handed it to him.

"That was fast."

"I'm not a stupid woman, Mr. Adams," she said and tossed some towels over his arm. "You'll need these, too."

"Thank you, Mrs. Philby."

She sniffed and said, "Just make sure that woman takes good care of that boy."

"I think she intends to, Mrs. Philby," he said, and then because of the look on her face added, "but I'll make sure she knows."

He left the kitchen and headed for Earl's room with the towels and water.

THIRTY-NINE

Clint stood back while Gloria cleaned Earl's wound and then rebandaged it.

"There," she said, "that should do it."

"Thank you, ma'am."

She helped Earl get comfortable in bed again, then took the bloody bandages and the pot and said, "I'll be right back. I'll take this back to the kitchen."

After she'd gone, Clint said to Earl, "Now that wasn't so bad, was it?"

"No, it wasn't . . . I guess."

"Earl."

"Yeah?"

"I've got to ask you if you know anything you're not telling me."

"Like what?"

"I don't know," Clint said. "That's why I'm asking you. Is there anything about what's going on up here that you'd like to tell me? Or anything you know you haven't told anyone?"

"Gee, Clint," Earl said. "If I knew somethin' helpful, I'd tell you. We're friends, ain't we?"

"Yeah, Earl," Clint said. "We're friends."

"You believe me, don't ya?"

"Yes, I believe you, Earl." He didn't add that he probably only believed him because he had a bullet wound in his shoulder.

He passed Gloria in the hall and she asked him to wait for her outside. He also passed Mrs. Philby, who gave him a long dirty look. He gave her a smile.

When Gloria came out of the house Clint said to her, "You and your friend almost killed me last night."

"Somehow," she said, with a sly smile, "I don't think you're really complaining. Hetty was a surprise?"

"A big surprise."

She reached a hand out to touch him, then had second thoughts and pulled it away. She looked around, as if checking to see if they were being watched.

"I asked my husband about you."

"Asked him what about me?"

"If he brought you here to hire you."

"And?"

"I honestly believe it never occurred to him."

"I'll have to trust your judgment on that."

"Then I asked him if he thought Bill Reddick would hire you. He said no to that, too."

Clint already knew that it had been Frank James

who sent for him, but he had to go along with the conversation.

"So if neither of the mine owners sent for me, who did?"

"I can't help," she said. "Did Hetty know anything?"

"No, but she's going to keep her ears open."

"That's good," she said. "I could introduce you to some of the other wives if you like."

"I don't think I'd survive," he said, "but you could talk to them for me." This had nothing to do with who had hired him, but with who might know that Frank Howard was actually Frank James.

"What should I ask them?"

He thought a moment.

"Just ask them if they've heard anything un- usual," he told her. "Anything that surprised them. Or if any of their husbands have been . . . talking about something."

"Something?"

"I'm poking around in the dark here, Gloria," he said. "I basically want to find out who shot at me and Earl and why."

"Okay," she said, "I'll see what I can do. Can you meet me at the shack later?"

"Probably," he said, "but not all night. I don't think Mrs. Philby would let me in tomorrow."

"She's basically a nice woman," Gloria said, "but you're right. We'll have to meet earlier."

"And don't tell Hetty."

She raised an eyebrow.

"You didn't enjoy your time with my friend Hetty?"

"I enjoyed it very much," he said. "Maybe you'd rather I meet her than you?"

"Uh, no," she said. "That wouldn't do. It's all right. Hetty just wanted a taste and I agreed that she could have one. But just a taste. The rest of the time you're in town, you're mine."

"What about your husb—"

"Don't worry about Jerrod," she said. "He has other things to worry about, like whether or not Bill Reddick hired you to kill him."

"You planted that little thought in his head?"

"Just to keep him busy."

Again, her hand went out to touch him, and she pulled it back.

"This is very hard," she said. "Not being able to touch you. Maybe we could go to the shack now?"

"My legs are still weak from last night, Gloria," he said. "I'm not as young as I used to be. I need time to recover. Besides, I do have plans for today."

"To find out who shot Earl?"

"To find out who shot Earl," he said, "among other things."

FORTY

The next person Clint wanted to talk to was Frank James. He went by Frank's shack, but it was empty. The door was open, though, so Clint went in just to be sure. He also checked the wooden chest where Frank had been storing his gun. The weapon and Holster were gone, and there was a smell of not only gun oil but also leather in the air. He left and pulled the door closed behind him. He went over to the Reddick Mining office to see if Frank was there.

The gun felt odd on Frank James's hip. Actually, it was on Frank "Howard's" hip, but it felt odd nevertheless. It had been a while since he'd worn it. In the beginning, he'd felt naked without it, but now he felt weighed down with it. Add the fact that this was Jesse's gun, which he had not yet worn, and it felt very strange.

When Frank entered the Reddick Mining offices

Bill Reddick looked at him and asked, "Since when did you start wearin' a gun to work? Or at all, for that matter?"

"I heard about poor Earl," Frank said. "Can't think of any reason somebody could have for wantin' to shoot him. If somebody's out there shootin' people for no reason, I want to be able to protect myself."

Reddick laughed.

"Can you even use that thing?"

"I can use it," Frank said and did not elaborate.

"Well," Reddick said, as if he hadn't heard him, "get Chapman to give you some pointers. He always wears one."

"Right."

"Or maybe Clint Adams, while he's in town."

"Yeah."

"Okay, forget about guns," Reddick said. "C'mere, we got a problem in shaft number three . . ."

Clint entered the office about a half an hour after Frank James did. Frank and Reddick were still huddled over some maps on Reddick's desk, and both looked up when he entered.

"Adams," Reddick said. "What can I do for you?"

"I was hoping to talk with Howard, here," Clint said.

"What do you need with Frank?"

"I understand he's sort of the law around here."

"Half the law," Reddick said. "We usually let both foremen take care of things. You'll want to talk with Derrick Kyle, too."

"I intend to," Clint said, "but I thought I'd start with Mr. Howard."

"Oh, all right," Reddick said. "I think we got this licked. Go ahead, Frank."

"Let's step outside," Frank suggested.

As they headed for the door Reddick laughed and called out, "Maybe you can teach Frank a thing or two about guns so he don't shoot his foot off."

"I'll see what I can do."

Outside Clint said to Frank, "If he only knew—"

"There's nothin' to know, Clint!"

"Okay," Clint said, "sorry."

Frank shook his head. "It's okay, I guess I'm just jumpy."

Clint frowned at the gun and holster Frank was wearing.

"That Jesse's Schofield?"

Frank looked down at his hip.

"Yeah, I couldn't part with it." He looked behind them at the door to the office. "Let's walk while we talk."

"Fine with me."

They walked in silence until they were totally out of earshot of the office.

"What's on your mind?" Frank asked.

"The law," Clint said. "Does Sheriff Buckles ever come up here?"

"He's been here once or twice," Frank said. "I usually try to avoid him."

"Why?"

Frank shrugged.

"Some lawmen have got great memories for wanted posters they've seen over the years. Just didn't want to take any chances."

"I can understand that."

"Were you thinkin' about gettin' him up here because of the shootin'?"

"The thought had crossed my mind," Clint said, "but—"

"Don't let me stop you," Frank said. "I can avoid him pretty easily just by stayin' up at the mine. If you think you need him, then send for him."

"Maybe I'll talk to Derrick Kyle first," Clint said. "Tell me what he's like."

"Pretty straightforward," Frank said, with a shrug. "Our bosses don't like each other and are competing, but we pretty much get along with one another."

"Does that mean you'd be willing to make the introduction?"

"Sure, why not?" Frank agreed. "Let's go over to the Augustus office and see if he's there."

They changed direction, Frank leading the way.

"What do you know about Kyle and his boss's wife?"

"Same thing I know about the boss's wife and anybody else," Frank said. "It's no secret that their marriage is not rock solid."

"So she sees him and other men?"

"As far as I know," Frank said, "she's sleeping with Derrick on the side and it's no secret, but I think he's the only one."

"Has she seen other men?"

"A miner or two," Frank said, "but never for very long, and never more than one man at a time. Just between you and me I think she's got some kind of arrangement with her husband."

That pretty much verified what Gloria had told Clint. At least he knew she wasn't lying about that.

"Frank, have you seen any new blood in town?"

"This ain't the kind of place fellas drift in and out of, Clint," Frank said. "That would be Ouray."

"That's what I mean," Clint said. "If there's a new face or two in town, chances are they're here for a reason."

Frank frowned. "I ain't seen anybody yet, but that don't mean somebody didn't drift in here yesterday or today. We might ask Derrick, though. He keeps his eyes open as much as I do—maybe more."

"More?"

"Well, I'm tryin' to keep folks from findin' out my real name," Frank said. "He's sleepin' with his boss's wife."

FORTY-ONE

When they reached the Augustus Mining office they lucked out. Derrick Kyle was just coming out, pulling the door closed behind him.

"I'd rather not talk to the old man if I don't have to," Frank was saying as they approached, and then he added, "Here's Derrick now," when he spotted him.

Derrick Kyle saw them, too, as he came down the stairs.

"Frank."

"Derrick."

"Who's your friend?"

"This is Clint Adams," Frank said. "Came to town yesterday with Earl and your man Chapman."

"That's right," Kyle said. "I heard Earl had a bullet in 'im. How's he doin'?"

"He'll be okay," Clint said. "Your boss's wife patched him up."

"Yeah, Gloria—Mrs. Augustus is good at that sort

of thing." Kyle extended his hand. "Pleased to meet you, Adams."

Clint shook the man's hand.

"Same here."

"What brings you to Red Mountain Town in the first place?" Kyle asked.

"You heard about Hangnil gettin' killed?" Frank asked.

"Yeah, I heard from Chapman."

"He was meetin' Clint in town to bring him up here."

"What for?"

"That's what he was going to tell me," Clint said. "Now I'm trying to find out on my own."

"How can I help?"

"I'm not sure you can," Clint said. "When I asked about the law up here I got your name and Frank's."

"We pretty much split the duty up between us," Kyle said. "We don't have any official standing, though. For that we'd have to send for Henry Buckles."

"That's what I told him," Frank said.

"You gonna send for Henry to find out who shot at you and Earl?" Kyle asked.

"Not yet. I've got a pretty good idea who it was: fella named Arvard Turner," Clint said. "Seems he shot Hangnil down in front of a saloon full of people. Now he might be after me."

"What for?" Kyle asked.

"I'll find that out when I find him."

"Well, I ain't seen hide nor hair of Arvard up here in a while," Kyle said.

"Then you do know him?"

For a moment Clint thought that Derrick Kyle looked annoyed with himself, as if he'd given up something he hadn't intended to.

"Everybody around here pretty much knows Arvard," he said. "He's always hangin' around, thinks he's pretty quick with that gun of his. Might be, for all I know. Speaking of guns, Frank. Why are you wearin' one?"

"Whether it's Arvard or not shot at Clint and plugged Earl," Frank said, "I don't aim to be next."

"Any reason why somebody would want to plug you, Frank?" Kyle asked.

"Not that I can think of," Frank replied, "but I ain't takin' any chances."

"I notice you wear a gun, Mr. Kyle," Clint said.

"Wore one before I got into the mining business, and I still do," Kyle said. "Besides, if we're the law up here, we need a gun once in a while. I'm surprised Frank, here, hadn't strapped one on a long time ago."

"Well," Frank said, "I'm wearin' one now."

"Wearin' it like you know how to use it, too, Frank," Kyle said.

"I can pull a trigger as good as the next man."

Derrick Kyle looked at Clint. "Anything else I can help you with?"

"Have you seen any strangers in town, either yesterday or today?" Clint asked.

"Can't say I have," Kyle said, "but I'll keep an eye out if you think it'll help."

"It wouldn't hurt," Clint said. "I'd be much obliged."

"No problem. If you don't mind, though, I've got some work up at the mine, right now."

"I won't stand in your way," Clint said.

"Frank," Kyle said. "See you later."

"Sure, Derrick."

As Kyle walked away Clint said, "He seemed real interested in the fact that you're wearing a gun."

"He did, didn't he?"

"Any reason you can think of for that?"

"Nope."

"Was he telling the truth about always wearing a gun?"

"Pretty much," Frank said. "I've always seen him with one strapped to his hip."

"Have you ever seen him use it?"

"No."

"It might be interesting to keep an eye on Mr. Derrick Kyle," Clint said.

FORTY-TWO

Al Maxx and Sam Burnett watched as Clint Adams and Frank "Howard" walked away from the Augustus Mining office.

"You really think it's them?" Maxx asked. "Jesse James's brother and the Gunsmith?"

"Unless somebody's makin' a big mistake," Burnett said. "But what the hell. Either way we make out."

"You think so?" Maxx asked. "You really think Arvard's got money to pay us for Adams?"

"I think Arvard better get some money to pay us for Adams," Burnett said. "And I know we'll be gettin' paid for Frank James. So yeah, I think we're gonna make out."

"So when do we make our move?"

"We gotta wait for the word on Frank James," Burnett said, "but nobody says we got to wait on the Gunsmith."

"You gonna brace 'im? Make him draw?"

"Naw," Burnett said. "We're gonna do this the easy way, Al."

"What's that?"

Burnett smiled.

"We're gonna bushwhack 'im."

Frank had some business at the mines. He and Clint agreed to meet later at the Saloon. They decided there was no harm in being seen together. As far as anyone knew Clint had only just met Frank, just as he had everyone else in Red Mountain Town.

Left on his own Clint took a turn around "town," which didn't take long. It was made up of shacks, tents and mud—and, in some cases, it looked as if the mud was keeping the shacks together.

Briefly, he gave some thought to the offer he'd received from Willie Dolan to go partners in his "cafe." He had to admit the young man's cooking was special, judging from breakfast. Under normal circumstances he would have gone back for lunch and supper just to be sure, but the mere fact that Willie had set up shop in Red Mountain Town was enough to deter Clint from putting his time and money behind the venture. Red Mountain was a boom town, and when the book was done, so too would be the town. Now, if Willie wanted to set up in a real town, where there was some future, that might change things. He decided to at least talk with him and give him some advice. If Willie was receptive to the advice, then maybe they'd talk about Clint possibly investing.

Clint still wasn't sure what his next move was going to be when he spotted Chapman coming down the street towards him.

"Hey, Chappy."

"Clint," Chapman said. "Makin' any progress?"

"Not much," Clint said, "mainly because I'm not quite sure what I'm trying to make progress towards."

"Finding Arvard Turner might be nice," Chapman said. "And the other fella he had with him when he was shooting at you."

"What are the chances Arvard came here?" Clint wondered aloud.

"I guess that depends on how bad he wants to shoot at you again," Chappy said.

"How well do you know Arvard, Chappy?"

"Well enough to want to kill him."

"Do you have any qualms about facing him with a gun?"

"I don't know what 'qualms' are, but if you're askin' me if I'm afraid of him, the answer is no."

"You're worried about how fast he is?"

"It don't matter how fast he is," Chapman said. "When I see him I'm gonna kill 'im—that is, if you don't do it first. And the way I see it, if we're both after him, he's as good as dead."

Clint had to agree.

"Where are you headed?" he asked Chapman.

"I wanna get some food," Chappy said. "I'm goin' to Eddie's Café."

"Eddie's?"

"One of the few places in town to eat."

"Is it good?"

"I like the food, and Hetty's a good waitress."

Ah, that was Eddie's!

"How about trying someplace new?"

"Like where?"

"I'll take you there," Clint said. "I had breakfast there and it was very good. It's run by a fella named Willie Dolan."

"Don't know 'im."

"Once you've had his food, you will."

If he couldn't commit to investing, the least he could do was bring Willie some new customers.

"He's with Chapman," Al Maxx said. "Now what?"

"Chapman knows how to use his gun," Burnett said. "That means we have to wait."

"Do we follow them?"

"This is Red Mountain Town, Al," Burnett said. "How far can they go? Let's get a drink."

"How about two drinks?" Maxx asked.

"Why the hell not?" Burnett asked. "Somebody else is gonna be payin' our tab soon, anyway."

FORTY-THREE

"Nobody's here," Chapman said as they entered Willie's tent. "The food must stink here."

"Nobody knows about it," Clint said. "That's why nobody's here."

"How did you find out about it?"

"By accident. Don't worry, the food's great."

Chapman looked doubtful, but followed Clint to a table.

"Kinda rickety," he said, as they sat down. The table rocked on its uneven legs.

"Come on, Chappy, this whole town is kind of rickety, isn't it?" Clint asked.

"You got a point there."

Willie came out of the kitchen and smiled when he saw his two customers.

"Hey, you're back," he said. "And you brought a friend."

"A hungry friend," Clint said. "What have you got for him, Willie?"

"Well, if he's really hungry I can make him a steak," the younger man said. "Or I've got some beef stew on the table."

"There's a chill in the air," Clint said. "Bring us two bowls of the beef stew. And start us out with a pot of that good coffee."

"Comin' up."

"What's your connection to this place?" Chappy asked.

"None," Clint said. "Like I told you, I ran into it this morning, by accident."

Willie came out with a pot of coffee and two mugs. He poured them full and then promised to return with two bowls of beef stew. Clint watched as Chapman tasted the coffee.

"Well?"

"It's not bad," the other man said. "In fact, it's better than Eddie's."

"Eddie is the cook at the other place?" Clint asked. "The fella with the big belly?"

"That's him," Chappy said. "Eddie Fawcett. He was the first one to put up a tent and start serving food."

"And who was second?"

"Well," Chapman said, "this place, I guess. Mrs. Philby and old Mrs. Davis, they feed their boarders, but Eddie was the only one servin' customers that I knew of until you brought me here."

Willie returned with the two bowls of stew and several hunks of fresh bread.

"You fellas need anything else, just lemme know."

Chapman took a hunk of bread, dipped it into the beef stew and stuck it in his mouth.

"This is delicious," he said and picked up his fork.

"I told you."

While they were eating, Chapman said, "You notice the way this Willie wears his gun, outside his apron?"

"I noticed."

"He hasn't always been a cook."

Clint shrugged.

"You haven't always been a miner."

"I get your point."

They finished their lunch and Willie brought out another pot of coffee.

"Did you think any more about my offer, Mr. Adams?"

"I, uh, haven't made my mind up yet, Willie."

"Okay," Willie said, "I won't press you."

Clint paid Willie for the food so they could leave as soon as they finished their second pot of coffee. He told Chapman the meal was on him because he'd picked the place.

"No argument from me."

After Willie left Chapman asked, "What offer?"

"He wants me to go partners with him in this place."

"Why don't you?" Chapman asked. "As soon as the word gets around, he'll have plenty of customers."

"But for how long?" Clint asked. "These mines have to peter out sooner or later. Besides, I'm only staying here long enough to find out what's going on."

"Have you talked with Howard and Derrick?"

"Both," Clint said. "Now I'm trying to decide if I need Buckles up here."

"What's he gonna do that you can't?"

"Nothing," Clint sad, "except wear a badge."

"I don't see that you need a badge-toter up here . . . yet," Chapman said.

"You might be right," Clint said. "I haven't made my mind up about that yet, either."

They finished their coffee and left.

"You going back to the mine?" Clint asked.

"Kinda," Chapman said. "I'm gonna go work my own claim for a while."

"You panning?"

"Some," Chapman said. "Doing some placer mining, too. You wanna come up?"

"No, thanks," Clint said. "I'd better stay here. I've got to meet Frank Howard at the Saloon soon."

"You and Frank are gettin' along," Chapman said. "It's almost like you guys know each other."

Clint watched Chapman walk away and wondered about his parting remark.

FORTY-FOUR

When Clint walked into the Saloon there was no sign of Frank James. He did, however, see two men sitting in the back who he had seen a couple of other times that day when they thought they weren't being seen. He went to the bar and ordered a beer.

In the back of the saloon, Al Maxx put his hand on Sam Burnett's arm and said, "There he is."

"Who?"

"Clint Adams," Maxx said. "He just walked in."

"Well, don't stare at him," Burnett said. "What's he doin'?"

"How can I tell you what he's doing if I don't stare at him?" Maxx asked.

"You can look at him without starin' at 'im, can't you?" Burnett demanded.

"He's at the bar, havin' a beer." Maxx looked at Burnett. "Do we take him now, Sam?"

"Does this look like a good place to bushwhack a guy, Al?"

"Well, no, but—"

"Then don't be stupid," Burnett said. "We're just gonna watch and wait for our chance. So you keep an eye on him now, without staring. Can you do that?"

"Yeah, yeah," Maxx said, "I can do that."

"And let me know what he does."

"Why don't you just turn around and look for yourself?"

"Yeah, then he'll never suspect that we're watchin' him, right?" Burnett asked. "Just do like I say, Al. Watch him . . . but don't stare!"

Sullenly, Maxx picked up his beer and tried to figure out how to watch and not stare at the Gunsmith.

Clint was still nursing his beer and watching the two men at the back of the saloon when Frank James walked in and joined him at the bar.

"Beer," he told the bartender.

"There's two men sitting near the back of the tent," Clint said. "Center table. Do you know them?"

Frank risked one quick look at the two men, which no one in the place caught—not even Al Maxx, who was looking directly at the two men.

"Never saw them before."

"Strangers in town?"

"Got to be."

"Well," Clint said, "they've been real interested in me."

"You, not me?"

"Well, they were watching you and me earlier, but then later I caught them watching me with Chapman."

"Well, either they recognized you," Frank said, "or you been pointed out to them."

The bartender brought Frank his beer.

"You know the two men in the back, Bud?" Frank asked. "Two strangers."

"They was here yesterday."

"Not before that?"

"They weren't in here before yesterday," he said. "Maybe they was in town, but not here."

"Did you see them with anyone yesterday?"

"That's funny."

"What is?"

"That you'd ask that." Bud, the bartender, touched his handlebar mustache. "Just yesterdays Arvard was in here."

"What was he doing?"

"Well, he was talkin' to them two," Bud said.

"What was funny about that?"

"He was filthy," Bud said, "covered with mud, and he slunk in here like he thought nobody could see him."

"But you saw him?" Clint asked.

"Hell, everybody saw him," Bud said.

"Okay, thanks, Bud."

The man moved down the bar to serve some other customers.

"They're either friends of Arvard's or he hired them," Frank said. "But I can't see him hirin' them."

"Why not?"

"Arvard wouldn't have the money."

"He might not need money."

"How's that?"

"Maybe he just told them who I am," Clint said. "Sometimes that's enough."

"So they're here for you, not me."

"Maybe."

"Maybe?"

Clint shrugged. "Could be somebody's lookin' to kill two birds with one stone."

"With them two bein' the stone," Frank said, "and you an' me bein' the birds."

"Right."

"Chances are they wouldn't try to take us together, though."

"So," Clint said, "one at a time."

"Question is . . ." Frank said.

". . . which one first?" Clint finished.

FORTY-FIVE

Clint and Frank finished their beers and ordered another each.

"They won't make a move while we're together," Clint said.

"So maybe we should split up and see who they go after," Frank suggested.

"Do we want to push them into making a move?"

"I vote yes," Frank said. "Let's get it over with. If they're after me, we can find out who sent them, and I'll find out who knows the truth about who I am."

There was still something for Clint to find out. He knew who had sent for him—Frank James. And he knew who had shot at him and hit Earl—Arvard Turner. What he didn't know was whether or not Arvard was acting on his own or for someone else, and the why of it, either way.

"Okay," Clint said, "let's leave together and go in

separate directions. Whichever of us isn't followed will double back and cover the other's back."

"Deal."

"Let's finish these beers, first," Clint said. "Our leaving has to look natural."

"I don't have any trouble finishing another beer," Frank said.

"Sam, they're movin'."

"What?"

"They're leavin'."

"Together?"

"Yeah. Should we follow them?"

Burnett gave it a few seconds of thought and then said, "No, let 'em go."

"But—"

"We get up and run after them now it'll be too obvious," Burnett said. "Besides, they may not split up outside."

"So we just let 'em go?"

"We let 'em go," Burnett said, then added, "this time. Finish your drink."

Clint and Frank split up outside, then doubled back when they realized they weren't being followed. They stopped short when they ran into each other.

"They didn't come out?" Frank asked.

"I guess not. Maybe I was wrong. Maybe they haven't been watching me."

"Or maybe they're too smart."

"Either way," Clint said, "nothing's going to happen now."

"So what next?"

"Don't you have a job to do?"

"Part of my job is to find Arvard Turner," Frank said, "and find out who shot Earl."

"What about Derrick Kyle?"

"Ben Hangnil wasn't his man," Frank said, "so he's not gonna be looking for Arvard. I also don't think he's too concerned about who shot Earl."

"So it falls to you?"

"Unless we send for Buckles. You make up your mind about that yet?"

"Who would we send?"

"Well, usually Earl would be used for an errand like that," Frank said. "I'd just have to send someone else. Maybe Chappy."

"Chapman can use a gun," Clint said. "Maybe we should keep him up here."

"Somebody should keep an eye on these two strangers," Frank said. "At least to find out where they're stayin'."

"You could use Chapman for that."

"That's a good idea," Frank said. "With Chapman on them we won't have to think about them so much."

"I guess we should check with him and see if he'll do it."

"I'm his boss," Frank said. "He'll do what I tell him."

"This has nothing to do with mining, though," Clint said. "It wouldn't be fair to ask him to risk his life—"

"Nobody's talkin' about fair, Clint," Frank said. "If life was fair, Jesse would still be alive and I wouldn't be here goin' by the name of Frank Howard."

Clint still didn't think it would be fair to put Chapman in this situation without a choice, but he decided not to argue with Frank at that moment.

"All we've got to do is find him," Frank added. "I can check and see if he's workin' a shift at the mine."

"He's not," Clint said. "I ran into him earlier and he said he was going to be working his own claim. Do you know where that is?"

"I didn't even know he had his own claim," Frank said. "We'll either have to find somebody who does know where it is, or wait for him to show up. And the chances are if I don't know he's got a claim, nobody else does, either. Up here men don't talk freely about that."

"Okay," Clint said, "so we wait for him to come back down. Meanwhile, we watch each other's back."

"Then let's go to my shack," Frank said. "We can watch them a lot better there than out here."

FORTY-SIX

Clint and Frank spent the rest of the afternoon passing a bottle back and forth and talking about Jesse James and the past. Clint would have preferred beer, but when Frank brought the bottle out to propose a toast to his dead brother, he could hardly refuse. From that point on, the bottle just kept going back and forth.

"Time to go lookin' for Chappy," Frank said, finally. But when he tried to stand up he fell right back down onto his ass. "Woops."

"You're too drunk to go out, Frank," Clint said. He'd been sipping while Frank had been chugging from the bottle. Clint felt the effects, but he wasn't drunk.

"Sh'all right," Frank said. "Gotta go." He was sitting on his bed, and at that moment he keeled over. By the time his head hit the mattress he was asleep. Clint wondered how many of Frank's afternoons were spent this way.

He undid his friend's gunbelt and hung it on the bedpost within reach. Just in case somebody came through the front door. He hated to leave Frank alone like that, but he had to go and talk to Chappy and check on those two strangers. Besides, a lot of days had gone by since Frank sent for him. What were the chances somebody would come after Frank today? It was still more than likely that whoever knew his true identity was going to ask for money. If they wanted to kill him they could have backshot him by now.

Frank left the shack to see if Chappy had come down from his claim.

The first place he looked was the Saloon, and that's where he found Chapman, standing at the bar with three men who looked familiar to Clint. As he approached he realized he had seen them with Chapman down in Ouray the first time they met.

He also scanned the room for the two strangers, but they were not there. It would have been easier if they were, since he was going to be asking Chapman to watch them.

"Hey, Clint," Chapman said, "Join us for a beer."

"Don't mind if I do."

Chapman introduced the other three men— Simms, Truman and Hanks.

The other three men finished their beer and said good-bye to Clint and Chapman.

"Was it me?" Clint asked, as the three men walked away.

"Actually, it was," Chapman said.

"What'd I say?"

"It's not what you said, it's who you are," Chapman assured him. "They don't want to be in the line of fire."

"Is the word out that I'm a target?"

"No, it's not that," Chapman said. "It's just that you're the Gunsmith. They figure somebody is gonna wanna try you. They don't want to be around when that happens. They're miners. They're not wearin' guns."

"Wearing a gun," Clint said. "That's what I want to talk to you about. Can we sit down?"

"Buy me another beer, and we can dance, if you want to," Chapman said.

"Thanks," Clint said, "but sitting down will be enough."

They sat and Clint talked, telling Chapman about the two strangers in town. He also told him what Frank Howard and he wanted him to do.

"I know the two you're talkin' about."

"You know them?"

"Well, no, I mean, I've seen them around," Chapman said. "They look like gunhands. You figure they're here for you?"

"I don't know who they're here for," Clint said, "but it looked to me like they were following me for part of the day."

"So you want me to watch your back?"

"We want you to watch them."

"I can understand why you want me to watch them,"

Chapman said, "but why does Frank want me to watch them?"

Clint realized he'd made a mistake.

"It's just that . . . well, he is sort of the law up here. He doesn't have the time to follow them around himself."

Chapman stared at Clint suspiciously.

"You know, I always thought Frank was hidin' somethin'," he said, finally.

"What do you mean?"

"There's just somethin' not right about him bein' up here," Chapman said. "What is it?"

"Seems to me that's the kind of question you ought to be askin' Frank."

"That's another thing," Chapman said. "You and him, you call each other by your first names like you been doin' it a long time. You fellas know each other from somewhere?"

"Chappy—"

"I know, I know," Chapman said, "ask Frank. Okay, I'll put that aside for now. Where are these two jaspers you want me to watch?"

"Now, we—I don't want you to brace them," Clint said. "There's two of them, and—"

"Clint," Chapman said, "I can handle myself. Just tell me where to find them."

"I don't know where they are right now," Clint said, "but I think it's a pretty sure bet that if you watch me for a while, you'll find them."

FORTY-SEVEN

Arvard Turner was tired of hiding like an animal. All he'd done was what he'd been hired to do and for that he'd been belittled and reduced to this. He was covered with mud and cold. He still had the money in his pocket that Derrick Kyle had paid him and there was no real law in Red Mountain Town. He decided it was time to get cleaned up and come out into the open. After all, he had Burnett and Maxx to back his play.

He decided to walk into town and stop at the nearest boarding house.

Jerrod Augustus looked up as Derrick Kyle entered the office.

"Adams isn't leaving town," he said to his foreman.

"Then he hasn't done what he came to do."

"Does he know why he was brought here?"

"I don't know."

Augustus chewed on a knuckle.

"What if Reddick brought him here to kill me?"

"Bill Reddick doesn't strike me as that kind of man, Mr. Augustus," Kyle said.

"Where's that little turd, Arvard?"

"I don't know," Kyle said. "He shouldn't be far, though. He's got somethin' to prove."

"He never should have killed that miner."

"I know that."

"But if he kills Adams," Augustus went on, "that would be a different story."

"If Arvard kills Adams he'll have to do it by shootin' him in the back," Kyle said.

"Is he still on the payroll?"

"I paid him off."

"Find him," Augustus said. "Offer him more money."

"He's not worth it."

"You just said all he has to do is put a bullet in Adams's back," Augustus said. "How hard can that be? If he gets himself killed while he's doing it, I don't care."

"He probably will—"

"Then he won't be able to point a finger at us . . . at you," Augustus said.

"Okay," Kyle said. "I'll find him."

"I want Adams gone," Augustus said, and as Kyle went out the door he muttered, "For more than one reason."

Burnett and Maxx were across the muddy road from the Saloon, where they'd seen Clint Adams go in alone.

"If he comes out alone," Burnett said, "we'll tail him and take him."

"We ain't gonna face 'im, though, right, Sam?" Maxx asked, nervously.

"That's what I said, Al," Burnett said. "There's no point in takin' any chances, and we still got Frank James to deal with."

"And then we find Arvard."

"And get paid."

"He better have the money," Maxx said.

Burnett looked at him. "He better have the money or know somebody who does," he said.

When Kyle left the office he stopped just outside. Where the hell was he supposed to find Arvard Turner now? He was in hiding after missing the Gunsmith and plugging Earl. Maybe, if he couldn't locate Arvard, he'd find somebody else who could do the job, but Red Mountain was full of miners, merchants, drummers and gamblers. Where was he supposed to find a gunman now, without going back to Ouray?

He decided there was only one place to look—the Saloon.

It was about that time that Gloria Augustus decided she'd had enough of trying to kill time. She was going to find Clint Adams and drag him to that shack so they could both build an appetite by ravishing each other. And this time she wasn't going to share him with Hetty. After that they'd get something to eat, and then go back to the shack. Unlike her husband she didn't care why Clint Adams had come to Red Mountain Town. She was just glad he was there, and she intended to make full use of him.

Clint stepped out of the Saloon and stopped just outside. He had immediately spotted the two men across the road and wanted to give them enough time to make up their minds. If they made their move now he'd have Chapman to back his play. It was a lot sooner than he'd figured, but at least Frank James was drunk and out of the way. He believed that you never really forgot how to use a gun, no matter how long it had been since you strapped one on, but Frank had never been the hand Jesse was with a gun, anyway.

Certain he'd given the two men enough time, he started to cross the road. That was when he saw Gloria Augustus coming toward him.

"Damn!" he said.

FORTY-EIGHT

"He's alone," Sam Burnett said. "Now we make our move."

Al Maxx drew his gun.

"No, no, don't pull that now," Burnett said. "Put it away before somebody sees you."

Maxx holstered his gun.

"Don't draw it again unless I draw mine. You got it?"

"I got it, Sam."

"Okay, then let's move."

Burnett stepped down into the street and then stopped so abruptly that Maxx walked into him from behind.

"Wait, damn it!" he hissed. "Who's that?"

"Clint!" Gloria called out. "Just the man I've been looking for. Can you guess why?"

"Not now, Gloria . . ."

"What?" she said, blinking as if she'd been slapped.

"Look behind me," he said. "Don't be obvious about it. Two men with guns. Are they following me?"

"There are two men and they're—no, they stopped, suddenly."

"That's because of you."

"What's going on?"

"I might have been on the verge of finding out who shot Earl," Clint said, "but I think you may have changed that."

"What should I do?"

"Well, for now," he said, taking her arm, "just walk with me."

Derrick Kyle came within sight of the Saloon and saw Clint Adams walking with Gloria Augustus, his hand on her arm. He didn't have to be hit in the head with a two-by-four to get the message. She had been avoiding him ever since Adams got to town, and now there she was, walking with him out in the open.

As they walked away he saw two men off to his right, both wearing guns, both watching Clint Adams.

"Do you two men know who that was?" he asked, approaching them.

He startled them, one almost pulling his gun.

"Easy," Sam Burnett said to Al Maxx. "Sure, we know. The Gunsmith. What's it to you?"

"How would you both like to make some money?" Derrick Kyle asked them.

• • •

From across the road Dan Chapman watched the entire tableau from the entrance of The Saloon. He knew the two men had been about to follow Clint when Gloria Augustus came along and changed things. Now he watched as Derrick Kyle stopped to talk to the two men. From the look on Kyle's face, it wasn't hard to figure out what they were talking about. Chapman knew, as did a lot of men in town, about Kyle and Mrs. Augustus. Seeing her with Clint couldn't be a pleasant thing for him.

Chapman stepped back so that he was just inside the tent. From there he watched and waited. When it became clear that the three men were going to come inside the saloon, he retreated even farther and took up a position at the bar.

"What the hell is going on?" Gloria asked as Clint whisked her around a corner and stopped. He peered out to see if anyone was following them. Nope. It looked like Gloria's appearance had changed their minds for sure.

"It's possible there was about to be some lead flying, and you were walking into the middle of it."

"Lead?" she repeated. "Bullets? Someone was going to start shooting at you . . . again?"

She looked to be upset at the prospect, but what he didn't know was that she was upset that someone was interfering with her plans.

"You should stay off the streets," she said, "and I

have just the place for you."

"Gloria," Clint said, "the street is actually where I need to be right now."

"No," she said, grabbing his arm, "you need to be with me, right now."

He grabbed her hand and removed it from his arm.

"Gloria, go home," he said. "I'll see you later."

"But—"

"Go," he said, and moved out into the street, again.

Derrick Kyle sat down with Burnett and Maxx after buying each of them—and himself—a beer.

"Am I correct that you two are for hire?" he asked.

"That depends on the job," Burnett said.

"But we already got—" He stopped talking abruptly when Burnett kicked him under the table.

"The job is the Gunsmith," Kyle said.

"Dead?" Burnett asked. "Or just gone."

Kyle hesitated a moment. His boss wanted Adams gone, but after seeing him on the street with Gloria, Derrick Kyle wanted him dead and said so.

"Can you do it?" he asked.

"Oh, we can do it," Burnett said. "All we need to do now is settle on a price."

FORTY-NINE

When Clint got back to the main street, the area in front of the Saloon was empty. There were some people walking by, but none of the ones he was interested in. He thought about going back into the saloon but he didn't want to be obvious about trying to draw the two gunmen out. Whether they were inside, or somewhere else, Chapman was probably on them. He decided to go and check on Frank James and see if he was still out cold.

When he got to the shack Frank was still sleeping off his afternoon drunk. Clint hoped that Bill Reddick wouldn't be looking for his foreman today. There wasn't much chance of getting any work out of him the rest of the day.

Clint made a pot of coffee for when Frank woke up, then helped himself to a cup. He carried it over to the bedpost, where the Smith and Wesson Schofield was hanging. He set the coffee down on a crate Frank was using as a table and lifted the gunbelt from the post. He removed the Schofield and set the holster aside.

The Schofield had been manufactured in 1875 to the specific refinements of Major George W. Schofield, who wanted a weapon he could load quickly, almost one-handed, while on horseback and in battle. Smith & Wesson liked the modifications and decided to mass produce the weapon. If Clint remembered correctly, they made nine thousand of them. Jesse had carried this one for a long time. It was heavy and reliable. Jesse was not a fast gun, nor was he a particularly good marksman, but he was cool under pressure and almost always hit what he was shooting at—maybe not with the first shot, but he hit it.

Clint slid the gun back into the holster and set the gunbelt back on the bedpost. He finished his coffee and decided to go and ask some questions that would help him find out who knew that Frank Howard was actually Frank James.

The first person to ask was the person who had hired him, Bill Reddick. He walked to the office of the Reddick Mining Company and did not run into anyone along the way—anyone he was interested in.

As he entered he saw Reddick standing hunched over his desk, staring down at some maps. He wondered if the man ever actually went down into the mine, where he sent his men.

Reddick looked up as he heard the door open.

"Adams," he said, "What is it? I'm busy."

"I wanted to talk to you about your foreman."

"Frank Howard?" Reddick stood up straight. "What about him?"

"How much do you know about him?" Clint thought the best tack to take was that he was suspicious of Frank.

"What do you mean?"

"When did you hire him?"

"Last year, some time."

"Why?"

"I needed a foreman."

"And he happened to walk in the door."

Reddick folded his arms and regarded Clint.

"As a matter of fact, that's almost the way it happened," he said. "Frank walked in one day. I had just lost my foreman the previous week. I'd interviewed some men but none fit the bill."

"And he did?"

"He had the knowledge I needed, and he seemed like he could handle men. I decided to give him a try."

"Did you ask him for identification?"

"What for?"

"To put him on the payroll."

"He told me his name and I put him on the rolls," Reddick said. "What's this about?"

"I was just wondering about his past. You just accepted that he was who he said he was?"

"Who else would he be?"

Clint shrugged.

"A man on the run, maybe?"

"If he is, I don't care," Reddick said. "He does the job. There could be a dozen men who are on the run and using phony names working for me and I wouldn't care, as long as they did the job. Does that answer your questions?"

"Pretty much."

"Where is Frank, anyway?"

"Last I saw him he said he had some work to do."

"Fine," Reddick said, leaning back over his maps. "That's what I pay him to do."

Clint didn't move, trying to think of some other questions. It seemed as if Reddick legitimately didn't know who Frank really was—and didn't care.

The mine owner looked up at him again and asked, "Are we done here?"

"Yes," Clint said. "Yes, we're done. I'm sorry I bothered you."

Reddick was concentrating on his maps again before Clint was out the door.

FIFTY

Clint stood just outside the door of Reddick Mining. Who else in Red Mountain Town would have had the opportunity to see Frank James and recognize him. One thing Reddick had alluded to made sense. There could be any number of men working for him who were on the run and living under an assumed name. Any one of them could have recognized Frank for who he really was. There was no way he could question every miner who worked for Reddick or for Augustus. They were going to have to wait for the blackmailer to make a move—if, indeed, blackmail was his ultimate goal.

Meanwhile, there was still Arvard Turner to catch and bring to justice, one way or another. Either turn him over to the sheriff for the murder of Ben Hangnil and the shooting of Earl, or have Dan Chapman kill him.

And then there were the two gunmen. Because he

was at an impasse as far as Frank James's problem was concerned, Clint decided that maybe a much more direct approach might work with them.

He walked over to the Saloon to see if they were there.

Burnett and Maxx had made their deal with Derrick Kyle and the Augustus foreman had left the saloon.

"Why didn't you wanna tell him we were already after Adams?" Maxx asked.

"Because he's gonna pay us to do a job we were already gonna do," Burnett said. "If Arvard pays us, then we get paid twice."

"And if Arvard don't pay us?"

"Then we get paid once, and Arvard dies."

"Do I get to shoot the little weasel?"

"Be my guest," Burnett said.

"What about that money this fella Kyle already gave us?" Maxx asked.

Derrick Kyle had given them an advance on what they'd get to kill the Gunsmith, and that resided in Burnett's shirt pocket.

"Don't worry about it," Burnett said. "I'll hold onto the money."

"But part of it's mine."

"You'll get your share, Al," Burnett assured him. "Don't tell me you don't trust me."

Maxx didn't speak.

"We're partners, right?"

"Right."

"Then don't worry about it," he said. "Come on, I'll buy you another beer."

Dan Chapman remained at the bar, nursing a beer. He had watched as money changed hands and it wasn't hard to figure out what for. He was trying to decide what his next move should be when he saw Clint Adams walk through the tent flap. He looked over at the bar and then came to join him.

"Beer?" Chapman asked.

"Yeah." Clint signaled for the bartender to bring two more cold beers.

"What happened with Gloria?" he asked.

"She got in the way."

"That's what women usually do . . . in my experience," Chapman said.

Clint looked at the man and said, "You and Gloria?"

Chapman grimaced.

"She tried, but I want this job," he explained. "I wasn't willing to risk it, not even for her. If I want some pussy I'll go down to Ouray and pay for it."

"I see our two friends are in here."

"And you just missed a third," Chapman said.

"Who?"

"Derrick Kyle."

"What was he doing here?"

"Hiring them."

"For what?"

"What do you think?"

"The way I figured," Clint said, "they already had that job."

"Maybe they're gonna get paid for it twice now."

Clint turned his head and looked over at the two men.

"What are you thinkin' of doin'?" Chapman asked.

"Havin' a talk."

"With them?"

Clint nodded.

"Want back up?"

"Yeah," Clint said, "but do it from here."

"Okay," Chapman said.

Clint started for the table, then decided to take his beer mug with him. He held it in his left hand.

"He's comin' over here!" Al Maxx said. He was almost in a panic.

"Relax, Al."

"But—"

"Just relax," Sam Burnett said, "shut up and let me do the talkin'. And remember what I said about your gun: don't go for it unless I go for mine."

FIFTY-ONE

"You fellas mind if I sit?" Clint asked when he reached the table.

"Depends on who you are, stranger," Burnett said, "and what you want."

"Well," Clint said, sitting anyway, "I think you know who I am. As to what I want, I just want to talk."

"Talkin's cheap enough," Burnett said. "What do you want to talk about?"

"So you do know who I am."

"You said I did," Burnett replied. "Who am I to call you a liar?"

"Then that gives you the advantage over me," Clint said. "What are your names?"

"I'm Al Maxx—" Al started, but Burnett cut him off.

"Why don't you tell us your business before we tell you our names?" Burnett suggested.

"Well, my business happens to be keeping you boys alive."

"That's a business I'd find worth talkin' about," Burnett said, "but why do you think our lives are in danger?"

"I think you've taken on a dangerous job," Clint said. "One I think you should have second thoughts about."

"What job would that be?"

"Is that how we're going to play it?" Clint asked.

Burnett spread his hands and said, "It's your game, Mr. Adams."

"Fine," Clint said. "I think somebody's put you boys up to trying to put a hole in me. That wouldn't be wise."

"Why's that?"

"Because I don't ventilate easy."

"Well, then, thanks for the warning," Burnett said. "Just who do you think put us up to this?"

"First? A little weasel named Arvard Turner. I don't know why you'd be doing it for him, though. He can't pay you, and you boys don't strike me as the kind who would risk their lives for a favor."

"He ain't got any mon—" Maxx started, but again Burnett shut him down.

"You said first," Burnett commented. "Who's second?"

"Fella named Derrick Kyle," Clint said. "But that one's harder to figure. I don't know why he'd want me dead. Maybe you boys can help me out on that one?"

"It's still your story."

"Well, then, it's either for himself out of jealousy," Clint guessed, "or it's for his boss."

"And why would his boss want you dead?"

"I don't know," Clint said. "If you can't tell me I might just have to go and ask him."

"You said jealousy," Burnett said. "You and him courtin' the same gal?"

"Something like that."

"Doesn't sound like a smart thing to do," Burnett said. "I mean, if he's gonna hire somebody to kill you over it. Why not just let him have the gal?"

"I guess that'd be up to her," Clint said. He sipped his beer and finally set it down on the table. The move seemed to make Al Maxx nervous.

"Well, I guess you fellas have told me all you're gonna tell me," he said.

"We ain't said much," Burnettt replied.

"That's true," Clint said, "but then, you haven't exactly denied much, either."

He stood up, causing Maxx to get even more nervous. Burnett, on the other hand, seemed calm.

"How about that name?" Clint asked.

"Why?"

"Because if you boys come after me I'm going to have to kill you," Clint said. "I hate killing men when I don't know their names."

Burnett regarded him silently for a few moments, then flicked a thumb toward his partner and said, "He's Al Maxx. My name's Burnett, Sam Burnett."

"Thanks," Clint said. He picked up his beer, turned and walked away.

As Clint walked away Maxx leaned forward and said urgently, "His back's to us, Sam. Let's take him now!"

"He's got cover, you idiot."

"What? Who?"

"See the fella at the bar?"

They both looked over at the bar, where Chapman lifted his beer mug to them.

"Who's that?"

"I don't know," Burnett said, "but we'd better find out before we make a move. Come on."

Clint had joined Chapman at the bar when Burnett and Maxx walked by them and headed out without a word.

"You talk 'em out of it?" Chapman asked.

"I doubt it," Clint said. "Especially not if they think there's money in it for them and a big rep."

"You know 'em?"

"Sam Burnett and Al Maxx." Clint said. "Never heard of them."

Clint put his elbows on the bar and sipped his beer. Chapman wondered idly just how many men Clint Adams had killed in his life without ever having heard of them before. And how many of them he still remembered?

FIFTY-TWO

When Clint left the saloon Chapman left with him. Together they surveyed the street.

"Looks clear," Chapman said.

"Yeah, it probably will be for a while."

"Why's that?"

"What I'd do if I was those two," Clint said, "is go back and renegotiate."

"Renegotiate."

"Sure," Clint said, "now that I know who they are they'll want more money before they come at me. We probably have until at least tomorrow."

"You wanna depend on that?" Chapman asked. "I could find a poker game, you know."

"No," Clint said. "It's just a theory. I don't want to bet my life on it, right now."

"Okay, then," Chapman said. "Where are we headed?"

"Let's go see if Frank slept off his drunk."

"Why?" Chapman asked.

"Well," Clint said, "they know who I am and I know who they are. But there's one other thing we accomplished today."

"What's that?"

"They know who you are, too."

"So?"

"So while you're watching my back," Clint said, "somebody's got to watch yours."

When they entered Frank's shack he was sitting up with a mug of coffee in his hand. With his other hand he snatched the Schofield from the table and pointed it at them.

"Whoa!" Chapman said. "Easy, Frank!"

Frank took a breath and placed the gun back on the table. With a shaky hand he raised the cup to his mouth. He looked like death warmed over.

"An afternoon drunk is the worst," he said.

"Coffee?" Clint asked Chapman.

"Sure."

Chapman walked to the table, sat opposite Frank and moved the gun out of his reach. Clint brought over a cup of coffee for Chapman and for himself.

"How are you feeling, Frank?" Clint asked.

"Lousy," he said, "What's been goin' on?"

Briefly, Clint told him what had gone on while he was . . . sleeping. He left out the part about him talking with Reddick about Frank, himself.

"Looks like you put them on the alert," Frank said. "They're either gonna make a move or pull up stakes."

"Clint thinks they'll try to get more money for the job," Chapman said.

"If they don't get it," Frank said, "they'll leave."

"That might not be a bad idea," Clint said. "In fact, I'd prefer it. Listen, you both know Augustus and Kyle. If Kyle's handing these fellas money to kill me, is it coming from him or his boss?"

"That depends," Chapman said, "on whether or not you're sleeping with Gloria Augustus."

"And if I have?" Clint asked. "It's her husband?"

"I'd say it's Kyle," Frank James replied, "but using her husband's money."

"Why would either of them want you dead, other than it being about Gloria?" Chapman wondered.

"There's no point guessing about it," Clint said. "Now that I've taken a direct route with Burnett and Maxx—and I've never heard of either of them— anyway, now that I've been direct with them, I might as well be that way with everyone."

"Which means?" Frank asked, obviously wondering if his past was going to be included in this new plan.

"Which means I'm going to go directly to the source and ask Derrick Kyle and Jerrod Augustus what they have against me."

"And when are you gonna do this?" Chapman asked.

"Right after my coffee."

Chapman smiled and said, "This should be interesting."

"What's this I hear about you workin' a claim?" Frank asked Chapman.

"Sure, why not?" Chapman asked. "A lot of the miners have their own small claims hereabouts."

"I just didn't know that you had one," Frank said. "Takin' much out?"

"Some," Chapman said. "I ain't gettin' rich, and I ain't a threat to Augustus or Reddick . . . yet."

"Hey, good luck with it," Frank said. "Somebody should give those two some competition. Maybe that's what they need to keep them from each other's throats."

"Well, if I can convince both of them that the other wouldn't hire a gun as part of this competition," Clint said, "maybe I can stop looking behind me."

FIFTY-THREE

Arvard walked into the Saloon and up to the bar. He'd gotten a room at one of the boardinghouses in town, had a bath and was clean and fed. Feeling more like a man than he had in days, he told the bartender, "Cold beer."

The bartender, a man named Clete, served him his beer and said, "The word's out on you, Arvard."

"What word?"

"They're lookin' for you for shootin' that miner in Ouray," Clete said, "and that kid, Earl."

"Yeah, well I'm lookin' for two men named Burnett and Maxx. They're supposed to be workin' for me. You seen 'em?"

"I seen two strangers, but I don't know their names."

Arvard gave him a description of the men he was looking for.

"I seen them talkin' with Derrick Kyle."

"Kyle? What's he talkin' to them for?"

"Beats me," Clete said. "Look, me and the other bartenders don't wanna be around you when the lead starts flyin', so why don't you drink up and be on your way."

"Yeah, yeah," Arvard said, "I'll be on my way—but only because I wanna be. This place stinks!"

He left his beer and went out the front flap of the tent.

Clint, Frank James and Chapman were walking past the Saloon when Arvard Turner came walking out.

"That's him," Chapman said. "That's Arvard."

"Don't call out," Clint said. "We don't want to spook him."

But it was too late. Arvard saw the three men and knew they had spotted him. He drew his gun and fired two quick shots, scattering the three of them to the ground, then took off on the run.

"Damn it!" Clint said.

The three of them got back to their feet and, covered with mud, ran after Arvard.

Sam Burnett and Al Maxx heard the shots as they were walking towards the Augustus mine office to find Derrick Kyle.

"Sounds like some action, finally," Burnett said.

"Should we go have a look?"

The door to the mine office opened and both Augustus and Kyle stepped out to see what the commotion was. They both saw the two men at the same time.

"No," Burnett told Maxx, "we got business here."

•　•　•

Arvard couldn't think of any place to run to except the mine office of Augustus Mining, where he figured to find Derrick Kyle. Hopefully, since Kyle was the man who got him involved in all this, he'd have a way to get him out.

"He's headin' for Augustus," Chapman said.

"Makes sense," Clint said. "They're probably the ones who hired him."

"I get the chance," Chapman said, "I'm puttin' a bullet right between his eyes."

Clint hoped he'd get a chance to talk to Arvard Turner before that happened.

As Arvard approached the Augustus Mining office on the run the front door opened. Instead of Kyle or Augustus, though, he saw Burnett and Maxx step out. This was perfect, he thought.

"Burnett! Maxx!" he shouted. "They're behind me. Clint Adams is behind me." He stopped just in front of the steps, out of breath and turned to look behind him.

"Good," Burnett said. "They can remove the body."

"Wha—" He turned and looked at Burnett just in time for the man to shoot him right between the eyes.

FIFTY-FOUR

Clint, Frank and Chapman stopped when they saw Arvard lying on the ground in front of the building. On the steps Burnett was just holstering his gun. Al Maxx was standing behind him.

Clint leaned over Arvard and saw that he was dead. He then looked up at Burnett.

"Did you a favor, Adams," Burnett said. "He was the one tryin' to hire someone to kill you."

"Is that a fact?"

Clint tried to see past Burnett into the office. There was no sign of Kyle or his boss, Jerrod Augustus.

"You gonna want some help movin' the body?" Burnett offered.

"You working for Augustus now, Burnett?" Clint asked.

"Me and Al, we been hired as . . . oh, you might say, security?" Burnett answered.

"I see."

"So I guess if you're not gonna need any help we'll just go on back inside."

"Why don't you do that," Clint said.

Maxx went into the office first, followed by Burnett, who closed the door behind him.

"Is this the kind of thing you and Kyle handle unofficially?" Clint asked.

"No," Frank said. "For this you'd need Sheriff Buckles."

"I didn't know this man," Clint said, "and I probably wouldn't have liked him, but I get the feeling he walked into a bullet without ever knowing what hit him, or why. That's no way for a man to die."

"What do you care how Arvard died?" Chapman asked. "Hey, he killed Ben Hangnil." Chapman pointed down at the dead man. "That's just how I woulda killed him."

"Dan, you wanna help me carry him to—"

"I ain't carryin' that piece of shit," Chapman said. "You fellas are on your own."

"Chappy—" Frank said, as the man walked away.

"Let him go," Clint said. "Turner killed his friend. We can carry the body. Where do we take it to?"

"We got a boot hill," Frank said. "It ain't much, but we call it ours. You want shoulders or boots?"

"I'll take his legs," Clint said.

"What are we gonna do about Augustus's new security men?"

"I guess we'll have to figure that out later."

* * *

They carried him to Red Mountain Town's excuse for a boot hill, a muddy bog. They had a brief discussion about how legal it would be to just bury him.

"Not legal at all," Clint said. "We should take the body down to Ouray and turn it over to Sheriff Buckles."

"Then he has to come up here, and there has to be an inquest," Frank said. "The way I heard it, Arvard gunned down Ben Hangnil while he was unarmed and in front of witnesses."

"That's how I heard it, too."

"Then let's just bury him and be done with it."

In the end they agreed. They dug what they hoped was a deep enough hole and dumped Arvard Turner's body into it. Then they started covering him up.

Standing over the grave, Frank leaned on the shovels he had gotten from the Reddick Mining office and said to Clint, "You don't suppose I'll be lucky enough that it was Arvard who recognized me?"

"That would be the lucky and easy way out," Clint said, "so I doubt it."

"So do I."

"Do you suspect anyone in particular?" Clint asked. "I mean, in the last couple of days have you formed any new opinions?"

"No," Frank said. "I have no idea, Clint. You?"

"All I think I can say for sure is I don't think it was your boss," Clint said. "We had a talk and he doesn't suspect you of anything, doesn't care if you're on the run—"

"Who told him I'm on the run?"

"Nobody," Clint said. "What he said was, he doesn't care who his men are or if they're on the run, as long as they do the job."

"Well, good," Frank said. "If there's one person I don't want it to be, it's Bill Reddick."

"You like him?"

"It's not about liking him," Frank said. "He said if the mine production went up in my first year as fore-man that I'd be in for a percentage. I can use the money."

"I see."

They each carried a shovel as they started walking away from boot hill.

"And I do."

"Do what?"

"Like him."

"Good for you."

They got back to the Reddick office and Frank re-placed the shovels without telling anyone what they had been for. When he came back out Clint had some questions.

"You said if production was up the first year . . . how many years does Reddick think this mine is going to produce?"

"He doesn't see it not producing," Frank said.

"And what about the Augustus mine?"

"Same thing."

"Wait," Clint said. "So you're telling me this isn't just a boom."

"Why do you think the railroad came into Ouray?"

Frank asked him. "These people are figurin' on set-tlin' here for good."

"Ouray . . . and Red Mountain?"

"And some of the other camps up here," Frank said. "These places are gonna turn into real towns, Clint. You didn't know that?"

"No," he said. "No one told me, and this just looks like a huge mud hole."

"It's gonna change," Frank said. "They're gonna elect a town council, a mayor—"

"And a sheriff?"

"Yes," Frank said. "That's why I want to get my percentage and get out of here, before that happens."

"When is all this supposed to happen?"

"Just as soon as Reddick and Augustus fight to the finish, I guess," Frank said. "The way I hear it, they each wanna be the first mayor of Red Mountain Town."

FIFTY-FIVE

In the Augustus office four men were sitting and talking, two on one side of the desk and two on the other. Derrick Kyle was standing beside his seated boss.

Kyle had explained to Augustus about Burnett and Maxx before the two men actually showed up looking for more money. Augustus had not been real happy about the new deal, but it had actually been his idea to get rid of Arvard.

"We won't need him goin' around talkin'," he told Kyle. "And if he gets caught, he's gonna talk."

"Agreed. It was my mistake getting' him involved—" Kyle was saying, when the door opened and Burnett and Maxx walked in.

They had announced their desire for a new deal and it was agreed they'd talk about it after they took care of Turner. Burnett was a happy man when he stepped outside the door and saw Arvard Turner running towards him. He'd drawn his gun and fired almost without thought.

Now, back inside after facing Clint Adams, Frank "Howard" and Dan Chapman, Burnett said, "Okay, Arvard's not a problem, anymore. Now let's talk about that extra money for the Gunsmith."

Augustus looked up at Kyle. Neither man had expected the Arvard Turner situation to be resolved so quickly.

Finally, the mine owner looked at the two men and asked, "How much do you want?"

Frank James was not recovered yet from his early drunk. Clint was surprised he was able to walk and talk at all, let alone help dig a grave, but the digging seemed to have done more to sober him up than all the coffee in the world might have done.

Of course, he still looked like hell.

"Well," Clint said, "it looks like if you and Derrick Kyle are the unofficial law up here, you're on opposite sides right now."

"If he hired those two gunnies to kill you," Frank said, "then he's not any kind of law."

They were back in Frank's shack, after stopping at Clint's room to get him a fresh shirt. There was nothing he could do about the mud on his pants except wait until it dried and try to brush it off.

"What do you think Jesse would say about you even being unofficially the law?" Clint asked.

Frank laughed. "Jesse'd find that funny as hell."

"Frank," Clint said, "why don't you just leave, instead of trying to find out who recognized you? I know what you said about your percentage, but really, when's that going to happen? Can you trust Reddick? Is it worth the risk?"

"It's worth the risk because I'm not wanted," Frank said. "I'm tryin' to go unnoticed for my own benefit, Clint, but the law don't want me."

"But you don't want to be around Buckles."

"Just 'cause I ain't wanted by the law don't mean I want to be around them."

"Well, look, I'm still in favor of the direct approach to solve my own problem, but that's not going to work for yours."

"I know. I'll back your play, Clint, and after that I guess you can leave any time."

"Well," Clint said, tucking in his new shirt after buttoning it, "I didn't ride all this way to stay two days and then abandon you. I've got nobody waiting for me."

"I appreciate it, Clint."

Clint stood up and looked down at himself. He and Frank had tried to wipe as much mud off themselves as they could before entering Frank's shack. It didn't help that much, though. The floor was covered with it. Still, Frank didn't seem so concerned about it. He hadn't even changed his shirt, just tried to brush it off the way he did his pants.

"If we take the direct approach now," Clint said, "we're going to have to face Burnett and Maxx."

"We don't know anything about them," Frank said, "but there's two of them and two of us."

"What about Kyle and Augustus?" Clint asked. "Can we expect any gunplay out of them?"

"Kyle wears one," Frank explained, "but I've never seen him use it. As for Augustus, I've never even seen him hold one."

"And if they're hiring guns they're not so willing to use one themselves," Clint said. "What about Chapman? Do we bring him in on this?"

"You trust him?"

"As much as you do," Clint said. "You know him longer, and better, than I do."

"I think he's pretty satisfied that Arvard Turner is dead," Frank said. "Why get him involved any more in our problems?"

"Okay, then," Clint said. "So we walk over to the Augustus office and see what happens?"

Frank stood up and said, "Let's go."

"How you doing?" Clint asked. "It's getting on towards dusk. We could wait until tomorrow, when you'll be feeling better."

"I'm sober," Frank said, "maybe not as a judge, but sober. Let's get it done. And the way I feel? Might be a blessing to have somebody put me out of my misery."

FIFTY-SIX

The four men in the Augustus Mining office had made their deal and now it annoyed Jerrod Augustus that the two hired guns were lounging around like they owned the place. They had even found a bottle of his good whiskey and were passing it back and forth without the benefit of glasses. The older man kept throwing his foreman dirty looks, as if to say, "If you had handled this in the first place we wouldn't need them."

"Don't you think you should be out there looking for Adams?" Augustus asked.

"Take it easy, Pop," Burnett said. "We'll take care of Mr. Gunsmith in our own time and in our own way."

"Seems to me you could have taken care of him about an hour ago, when he was here," Augustus said.

At that moment the front door opened, attracting the attention of all four men. An angry Gloria Augustus came storming in, slamming the door behind her.

"Well, well," Sam Burnett said, "what have we here?"

Gloria stopped short and looked at Burnett. He was tall, wide-shouldered and good-looking, and he had some of the danger about him that Clint Adams had. She was still angry at Clint for brushing her off so abruptly earlier in the day. Perhaps she was looking at a likely replacement.

"Jerrod," she said, "we have guests."

"More like new employees, ma'am," Burnett said, standing up. "And who might you be?"

"This is my wife, Mr. Burnett," Augustus said, "and I'll thank you not to look at her that way."

"This is your wife?" Burnett asked, in disbelief. "Well, Pop must have more fire in his furnace than he looks."

"Not necessarily," Gloria said. "Aren't you going to introduce us, Jerrod?"

"This is Mr. Burnett and Mr. Maxx."

"Sam Burnett, ma'am," Burnett said, removing his hat, "and it's a real pleasure."

Gloria came forward so she could give the rough-looking man her hand. Derrick Kyle was watching the whole thing with a dissatisfied look on his face. It was bad enough he had to compete with Clint Adams, now there was this man.

But no one had time to examine the situation because at that moment someone called out from outside, "Hello in the office!"

The four men exchanged a glance while Gloria was the one to go to the window to see who was there.

"It's the Reddick foreman, Frank Howard, with Clint Adams," she said. "Does he want to talk to you, dear?"

"I think he wants to talk to these two gentlemen," Jerrod Augustus said.

Al Maxx tossed a quick look at Burnett. This was not what they had in mind. They were supposed to bushwhack Adams and take him from behind.

"I think your foreman should go out and talk to them first," Burnett said.

"But we hired you—"

"Not to talk, Kyle," Burnett said. "That's your job."

"Fine," Kyle said, "I'll talk to them."

As Kyle headed for the door Burnett looked at Augustus and said. "You got any rifles in this place?"

Clint and Frank James watched as Derrick Kyle came out the front door.

"What's goin' on, Frank?" he asked.

"I think you're in a little trouble, Derrick," Frank said.

"What kind of trouble?"

"The bad kind," Clint said. "You and your boss have hired somebody to kill me. I don't take kindly to that, Derrick, so either go for that gun you're wearing, or send your hired killers out here."

"Whoa, wait, wait," Kyle said, raising his hands, "I'm no gunman and I'm not payin' anybody. You'd better talk to Augustus about that."

"You paid Arvard Turner to kill Hangnil, didn't you?" Frank asked.

"Not to kill him," Kyle said. "Just to keep him away from Adams."

"Why?"

"We knew that somebody had sent for Adams and was sending Hangnil down to Ouray to fetch him and bring him back."

"Why did you care about that?"

"He's got a big rep as a hired gun," Kyle said. "My boss thought your boss was going to hire him."

"That's stupid," Frank said. "Augustus and Reddick are two businessmen. Nobody ever said anything about bringing a hired gun in."

"Hey," Kyle said, "he's the boss."

"And now you've hired these two," Clint said.

"Not me, Augustus," Kyle said. "I'm just a mine foreman doin' his job."

"Better send those two out here, Kyle," Clint said, again.

"Wait, wait," Kyle said. "I-I'll try."

"Looks like your foreman is sellin' you out, old man," Sam Burnett said.

"Son of a bitch," Augustus swore.

"What's going on, Jerrod?"

"Shut up, Gloria," her husband said. He looked at Burnett. "I'll throw in some extra money for Kyle, Burnett. He's a traitor. You take care of him along with Adams and you can have his job."

"Foreman?" Burnett asked. He looked over at Gloria. "I wonder what else comes with that job."

Gloria Augustus actually smiled at him.

"Al," Burnett said. "Kill that foreman first chance you get."

Burnett moved quickly to one of the windows with a borrowed rifle in his hands.

Kyle turned and put his hand on the doorknob to open the door, but before he could there was a shot. A chunk of hot lead tore out a piece of the door and punched him in the chest. As he was flung off the porch one of the windows broke, a rifle barrel poked out and more shots were fired. Clint heard a grunt next to him as he dove, slammed into Frank James and brought him to the ground with him.

FIFTY-SEVEN

Clint took Frank to the ground with him and then rolled, grabbing for his gun at the same time. He had to leave Frank to fend for himself. There were now two broken windows, and two rifles firing at them. The two gunmen inside had obviously decided not to do things face-to-face. And, for some reason, they had either decided or been told to take care of Derrick Kyle, as well. It was possible—and probable—that Augustus simply thought everyone was against him, and he was trying to solve his problems all at once.

Or else the gunmen themselves had taken over.

Inside the office Burnett called out to Maxx, "Hold your fire."

Maxx stopped shooting and waited. Outside, the two men were scrambling for cover.

Burnett turned to Augustus and asked, "Is there a back way out?"

"Well, yes, but—"

"Good," Burnett said, "we're gonna use it, unless we can make a new deal right now!"

"We just made a new deal—"

"Well, I want a newer one," Burnett said.

"How much do you want?"

"Half."

"Half?" Augustus asked, not understanding. "Half of what?"

"Half of everything, old man," Burnett said. "Half of everything, or we're out the back door and we'll leave you to face the Gunsmith—and Frank James."

"Frank . . . who?"

"James," Burnett said, "brother of Jesse James."

"I don't understand—"

"Then you'd better pick it up real quick," Burnett said. "Frank Howard is really Frank James, and right now he's out there with the Gunsmith, and they're kinda mad."

"The Gunsmith and Frank James?" Augustus asked. "How can I be sure you can even handle them? There's only two of you."

"You don't know it," Burnett said, "but you're gonna have to pay to find out!"

"I think I want to leave—" Gloria started.

"Oh, no, missus," Burnett said. "You're not leavin'. You're a big part of this."

"I don't want any part of it!" she said.

"Too late." Burnett looked at Jerrod Augustus. "Make up your mind, old man. Are we partners or not?"

FIFTY-EIGHT

"Frank?"

Clint and Frank had managed to put some distance between themselves. Each was facedown in the mud—again.

"Frank, you hit?"

"Nicked," Frank called back. "You?"

"No."

"Was this the direct approach you were talkin' about?" Frank asked.

"Not exactly—"

Clint stopped short when the front door opened. He looked around. Apparently, no one had been attracted by the shooting, or no one wanted to be.

He saw Gloria Augustus first and then Sam Burnett right behind her. He had one arm around her waist, in the other hand his pistol.

"Adams? Can you hear me?"

"I can hear you and see you, Burnett," Clint called back. "Let the woman go."

"Oh, no." Burnett tightened his hold on Gloria's waist. "I like her. We're just startin' to get close. Although I will kill her if you don't toss your gun out where I can see it."

Clint studied the front of the building for a moment. Burnett in the doorway with Gloria, a rifle barrel still sticking out one window, presumably being held by the other man, Maxx. Augustus was probably under a desk somewhere.

"Come on, Adams," Burnett shouted. "Get rid of your gun and put your hands up. You, too, Mr. James."

So, Burnett knew that Frank was Frank James.

"We can't do that, Burnett."

"Why not?"

"It's simple," Clint said. "As soon as we're unarmed you'll kill us."

"You think I would gun down two unarmed men?"

"I think that's exactly what you plan on doing."

"If you don't get rid of your guns," Burnett said. "I'll kill 'er."

"Clint?" Gloria's voice quivered. "Do as he says. Help me."

"I'll help you, Gloria," Clint said, "but I won't die for you. No deal, Burnett. Come up with something else. This isn't going to work."

Burnett was confused. This was supposed to work. Threaten the woman, disarm Adams and Frank James, then kill them. It was a sound plan.

Why wasn't it working? He didn't have a backup plan.

Al Maxx was nervous and about to panic. Should he fire? But fire at whom? Both Adams and Frank James were flat on their stomachs in the mud. There were so many ruts in the road it was as if they were in trenches. There was no clear shot.

He started to think about the back door.

Jerrod Augustus was, indeed, huddled beneath his desk, just in case lead started flying inside the office. He was wondering what he was going to do if this didn't work out. If Adams lived he'd be after him, and if Burnett lived he'd have the man as a partner.

He would have liked things back the way they were before he'd heard that Clint Adams was coming to Ouray and asked Derrick Kyle to find out why.

At least Kyle was dead. He wouldn't be sleeping with Gloria, anymore.

Frank James had been about to toss his gun away to save Gloria Augustus when Clint told Burnett that they wouldn't be doing that. He was right. Burnett and the other man would not hesitate to shoot them down once they were unarmed.

Being on this side of the law was a lot different. He was going to have to let Clint make all the decisions.

Gloria Augustus cursed all men. Her husband for bringing her to this godforsaken place. Derrick Kyle for not being man enough to take her away. Clint Adams for probably being the reason she was in this situation. And the brute who was holding her so closely she could feel his erection through his trousers, fitting right into the cleft of her ass. Under other circumstances she would have enjoyed it, but being on the verge of death detracted from the thrill.

Somewhat.

Clint knew he was signing Gloria's death warrant, but he was not about to allow himself to be shot down, unarmed, not even to save an innocent woman. Besides, he wasn't all that sure how innocent she was in all this.

FIFTY-NINE

Everyone was frozen in the moment and it fell to Clint to make the first move.

"Come on, Burnett," Clint said. "Show everybody what a man you are. Step out from behind the woman and face me."

Silence.

"You're not the one callin' the shots here, Adams!" Burnett shouted back.

"Well, somebody has to," Clint said. "You sure are doin' a piss-poor job of it."

"I'll put a bullet in her!" Burnett screamed. "I swear I will."

"We've been through this already, Burnett," Clint said. "You kill her, we kill you. And right now you've only got us to deal with. Any minute there'll be some more men with guns here to see what all the shooting was about. So make up your mind. Do something, for Chrissake."

Clint closed his eyes. He hoped he wasn't pushing the man to actually put a bullet into Gloria.

"Okay," he said, "look, I'll stand up, okay?"

Clint got to his feet slowly. He gave one look at the rifle barrel sticking out the window, then told himself to forget about it. He only hoped that Frank would know enough to watch the rifle while he dealt with Burnett.

Clint walked slowly toward the building. Burnett had Gloria in front of him, arm around her waist, but in order to see Clint he had to move his head to the side. Clint just needed a large enough target to shoot at. It was getting darker out, and if darkness fell on them this was going to be a lot harder.

"Come on, Burnett," he said. "Take a shot."

The man would have to move his head a lot to get a good look at Clint to shoot him. That was all he needed. Or if Gloria would cooperate and start struggling, even that would help.

"Look, big man," Clint said. "I'll holster my gun." He did so, and hoped that wouldn't be the last foolish decision of his life. "Come on, what more could you want?"

From the window he heard Al Maxx say, "Take the shot, Sam."

"Yeah, Sam, take it!" Frank James chimed in.

Gloria didn't know what was going on, but she shouted, "Take the shot, damnit! Be a man!"

Somehow, when a woman belittles you it stings more. Burnett felt that sting. He jerked his head to his right so he could see Clint with both eyes and raised his gun.

Clint drew in one unbelievably swift motion and fired. Later both Frank James and Gloria would say they never saw the move. All Gloria knew was that something hot whizzed by her cheek. She heard it strike flesh, then felt something warm on the side of her face and on her shoulder. The arm around her waist went slack and, as she stepped away quickly, the body of Sam Burnett fell forward.

"Jesus!" she screamed.

Frank knew the man in the window was his. He only had to wait his turn. He never saw Clint draw, but there was a shot and Sam Burnett fell forward. The man in the window leaned out to watch the action. Frank aimed Jesse's Schofield and fired once. The bullet struck the man on the top of the head, driving him back inside with a thud.

Unless Jerrod Augustus was waiting for them inside with a gun, it was over.

Clint stepped around the body of Derrick Kyle and mounted the stairs. Next he checked on Burnett to make sure he was dead. Only then did he look at Gloria, who was shaking uncontrollably. She had Burnett's blood and gore on her face and shoulder. Clint's bullet had struck him in the right eye, exploding as it continued on through his brain and out the back of his head.

"Blood," she said, looking at her hands. She had tried wiping it off. "Blood . . . is it mine? Am I shot?"

"You're fine, Gloria," he said. "The blood is Burnett's."

"I'm not shot?" she asked.

"No."

She stepped forward and slapped him. Leaving a bloody handprint on his cheek.

"You were going to let him kill me!"

"I was not—"

"How could you take that shot?" she demanded. "Jesus, I felt the bullet go right by me. How could you even make a shot like that?"

"I didn't have a choice."

Frank had mounted the steps and gone to the window. He leaned in, then back out.

"This one's dead, too."

"Where's your husband?" Clint asked Gloria.

"If I know Jerrod," she said, wiping her hand on her dress, "he's hiding underneath his desk."

"Let's go inside and see," he said, taking her by the arm and guiding her through the door. "We've got some questions for him."

SIXTY

Word got around Red Mountain Town pretty quickly that Frank Howard was actually Frank James. The thing that surprised Frank was . . . nobody cared. Least of all Bill Reddick.

"Like I told your friend Adams," the mine owner said, "as long as you do your job I don't care what your real name is. Besides, I'm gonna need you even more now that Augustus is in a state of disarray."

The word also got out that Augustus was hiring gunmen, and that he had gotten his own foreman killed. After that some of the miners working for him switched over to Reddick's operation, and some of them simply left.

Most of this happened the next day, after Clint and Frank had hauled Augustus out from underneath his desk to ask him what the hell was wrong with him?

"You and Reddick were competing fair and square," Frank had told him. "One of you would have ended up mayor of Red Mountain, eventually. Why would you bring gunmen into it?"

"I thought it was Reddick who was bringing in a gunman when I heard that someone was sending for Clint Adams."

"Me sendin' for Clint was somethin' personal," Frank had told Augustus. "It had nothin' to do with Reddick or his mining operation. You made a foolish mistake, old man, and cost the lives of five men."

Seven, Clint had thought, if you counted the two other men Arvard had roped into helping him.

Clint decided that when he got back to Ouray he'd tell the whole story to Sheriff Buckles. Let the lawman decide if he had grounds to arrest Jerrod Augustus.

He spent the night in his boardinghouse room after checking on Earl's progress. The boy was up and about a lot sooner than anyone thought he would be. Still, Clint didn't think he should try riding down the mountain so soon.

"Would you stop and see my sister and tell her I'm okay?" Earl asked.

Remembering the last time he had seen Earl's sister, Clint said, "It would be my pleasure."

Later that night there was a knock at Clint's door. He didn't answer it. He felt certain it was Gloria Augustus, and he didn't want to see her. The person didn't knock again and, after a few moments, he heard them walk away.

He felt sure his actions would meet with the approval of the landlady, Mrs. Philby.

• • •

Clint woke several mornings later with Lindy, Earl's sister, down between his legs. She had begun by touching his flaccid penis with her fingertips, just sliding them up and down the underside, watching with fascination as it swelled and grew. As it began to crawl up Clint's belly, he stirred and by the time he woke she was licking him.

"Mmm," he said, "nice way to wake up."

"You think that's nice?" she asked and engulfed him in her mouth. It had been established days ago that Lindy loved his penis. She said so many times, while licking and sucking it. She said it was the prettiest, tastiest one she'd ever had, and if he stayed in town a few more days she'd make it worth his while.

True to her word she made it worth it every night, and every morning, and this morning was no different. She suckled it, and made love to it, until it was ready to burst then climbed on top of him, stuffed it inside her and rode him until he exploded. She fell on him, then, kissing him, sucking his tongue furiously and doing something to him with her insides that amazed him. It felt like a wet, velvet glove was pulling on him. She had done this to him for the past two mornings and the result was always the same—he got hard again, inside her. She then rode him even longer than before, moaning and crying out, biting her lips and scratching his chest until finally she shuddered, stifled a scream and fell atop him again, this time to rest.

The first time, she said, was for him.

The second was for her.

• • •

By the fourth day Clint was ready to leave. He thought if he stayed any longer Lindy might give him a heart attack. That morning, after saying good-bye, he started for the livery stable and stopped when he saw two riders he recognized coming towards him on the main street.

"Clint!" Earl called out.

He stopped in the street and allowed Earl and Frank James to catch up to him.

"How're you doing, Earl?"

"I'm feeling much better," Earl said. "Did you tell my sister I was okay?"

"I did."

"How did she take the news that I got shot?" he asked. "She's real protective."

"She was upset," Clint said, "but I did my best to console her."

"I appreciate it," Earl said. "I'd better go tell her I'm back. Are you leavin' town?"

"I'm plannin' on it."

"Well, it's been a real pleasure knowin' ya," Earl said. He reached down from his horse to shake hands. His grip wasn't quite as firm as it should be yet, but he was recovering.

"Take care, Earl."

The young man turned to Frank James and said, "Thanks for ridin' down with me, Mr. James."

"Sure, kid," Frank said. "Don't mention it."

As Earl rode away Clint noticed that Frank's horse had a bedroll on it.

"Where are you headed?"

"Leavin'," Frank said. "I thought you'd be gone by now."

"No," Clint said, "I managed to find something to keep me here a few more days."

"Headin' for the livery?" Frank asked.

"Yep," Clint said. "Gonna saddle up."

"Mind if I tag along?" Frank asked. "I mean, to the livery and when you leave."

"Come on," Clint said. "I could use the company."

Frank watched while Clint saddled his Darley Arabian and then the two men rode out of Ouray together.

"Mind if I ask why you changed your mind about staying?" Clint asked.

"I don't mind," Frank said. "I had to kill another man. Figured I better leave after that. One too many, you know?"

"Anybody I know?"

"Yep," Frank said, "Chapman."

They rode along in silence for a while.

"That make a difference to you?" Frank finally asked. "I mean, I know you liked the fella."

"Why'd you kill him?"

"He was the one who recognized me," Frank said. "Said Jesse and I killed his brother in some town in Kansas. Worked in a bank."

"You remember the fella?"

"Naw," Frank said. "We robbed a lot of banks, Clint."

"I know."

"He wouldn't let it lie," Frank said. "Drew on me and

I had to defend myself. Figured I better leave after that.
Mr. Reddick was good enough to give me some gold."

"A lot?" Clint asked.

"Enough."

"Well, that was good, anyway."

"Yeah."

They rode along in silence a bit longer and then
Frank said, "I get tired of the killin' but it don't seem
to ever stop."

"I know what you mean, Frank," Clint said. "I've
had enough of it, myself."

Giant Westerns featuring The Gunsmith

Little Sureshot and the
Wild West Show
0-515-13851-7

Dead Weight
0-515-14028-7

J799

Penguin Group (USA) Online

What will you be reading tomorrow?

Tom Clancy, Patricia Cornwell, W.E.B. Griffin,
Nora Roberts, William Gibson, Robin Cook,
Brian Jacques, Catherine Coulter, Stephen King,
Dean Koontz, Ken Follett, Clive Cussler,
Eric Jerome Dickey, John Sandford,
Terry McMillan, Sue Monk Kidd, Amy Tan,
John Berendt…

You'll find them all at
penguin.com

*Read excerpts and newsletters,
find tour schedules and reading group guides,
and enter contests.*

Subscribe to Penguin Group (USA) newsletters
and get an exclusive inside look
at exciting new titles and the authors you love
long before everyone else does.

PENGUIN GROUP (USA)
us.penguingroup.com